DIESEL

SATAN'S FURY MC

L. WILDER

DEDICATION

To Natalie-
Thank you for all you do, but mostly for being such a wonderful friend.
(And FYI- You were right about Diesel's cover!)

Diesel
Satan's Fury MC
Copyright 2018 L. Wilder
All rights reserved.

L. Wilder www.lwilderbooks.net

Cover Model: Virgil Aubriot

Cover Design: Mayhem Cover Creations
www.facebook.com/MayhemCoverCreations

Editor / Formatter: Lisa Cullinan

Teasers & Banners: Gel Ytayz at Tempting Illustrations

Personal Assistant: Natalie Weston PA

– Other titles in the Series –

Catch up with the entire Satan's Fury MC Series today!

All books are FREE with Kindle Unlimited!

Summer Storm (Satan's Fury MC Novella)

Maverick (Satan's Fury MC #1)

Stitch (Satan's Fury MC #2)

Cotton (Satan's Fury MC #3)

Clutch (Satan's Fury MC #4)

Smokey (Satan's Fury MC #5)

Big (Satan's Fury #6)

Two Bit (Satan's Fury #7)

Damaged Goods- (The Redemption Series Book 1- Nitro)

Max's Redemption (The Redemption Series Book 2- Max)

You can also check out the Devil Chasers in the new Boxed Set!!

My Temptation: The Happy Endings Collection

Bring the Heat: The Happy Endings Collection

His Promise: The Happy Endings Collection (Boxed Set coming soon!)

❀ Created with Vellum

PROLOGUE

Scotty

AS A KID, I never knew much about my father—in fact, not a damn thing. I figured that my mother would've, at least, given me some small pieces of information about him if she thought he was even the slightest bit worth it. Instead, I convinced myself that he was just some deadbeat dad who'd left her in the lurch. A real man would've taken care of his kid regardless of what kind of relationship he had with his mother, so I decided he was better off kept in the shadows. He remained there the entire time I was growing up as I tried to pretend that neither his identity nor his actual existence bothered me. When I was three, Mom married Carl, and the pretending became a little easier. Carl was a good guy: kind-hearted and easygoing. He was older and already had kids from a previous marriage, so he had no problem adding one more.

Together, they worked their asses off to make sure that I had everything I could possibly need, and I don't mean by putting a roof over my head and clothes on my back, they loved me and made damn well sure I knew it.

Overall, I had it pretty good growing up. I was happy, but thoughts of my father were always in the back of my mind. Every time I looked in the mirror, I wondered if I had his eyes, his build, or if I looked *anything* like him at all. It was the nature of the beast to be curious about the man who had something to do with bringing me into this world. I often wondered if he would've been proud of how I'd turned out. By the time I had turned twenty-four, I figured I'd never find out, but that all changed when my mom got sick. She'd given her fight with cancer everything she had, but in the end, it got to be too much for her.

Things were looking bleak, and we all knew we could lose her at any time. After a long night at the shop, I came home and found Carl sitting on the front step with a beer in his hand. He wasn't one to drink, so I knew it had been a bad night. "She's been asking for you."

I patted him on the back and started towards her room. When I walked in, it was completely silent as the nurse hovered over her; suddenly, I worried that I'd gotten there too late. "Is she …"

"No, sweetheart. She's still holding on," she warmly replied as she made her way over to me. "She's been waiting for you to get home."

Dread washed over me as I looked towards her bed. Seeing my mother's frail, ashen body made my heart ache in a way that made it hard to breathe. I walked over to the edge of the bed and took her hand in mine; she was just skin and bones. I leaned towards her and whispered, "Hey, Momma. It's me, Scotty."

Her eyes slowly flickered opened as she turned to look at me. Her voice was weak and strained as she mumbled, "I need you to go ... over to my jewelry box ... Bring it to me."

"What for?"

"Just ... bring it to me, Scotty."

"Okay, Momma." I walked over to her dresser, retrieved the small wooden box, and brought it back to her. "Here. I've got it."

"Open ... the bottom drawer"—she watched me intently then took a deep breath—"and look under the fabric."

I did as she asked and found an old photograph hidden beneath the bottom layer of red velvet fabric. Carefully, I picked it up and studied the picture of a man who was standing next to a motorcycle. He looked to be about my age with shaggy, blond hair, and he was wearing a leather vest and jeans. The photograph was faded and yellow and looked like it was at least twenty years old. As I sat there staring at it, it quickly dawned on me that it was a picture of my father. I flipped it over and noticed a name and address written on the back and then looked over to Mom. "Is this really him?"

"Yes, sweetheart. That's your father." She sighed. "You should know ... he doesn't know about you, Scotty."

"What?"

She placed her hand on mine as she continued, "I was young and naïve. He never loved me the way I loved him, Scotty. When he met Melinda ... he fell head over heels for her ... and forgot all about me. I was embar-

3

rassed ... I couldn't bring myself to tell him that I was pregnant."

"So, he never had *any* idea about me?"

"No, sweetheart. I left town ... as soon as I started showing." A tear trickled down her cheek. Listening to her say that he had no idea I was his son felt like the rug had been pulled out from under me.

"Why are you telling me this now?"

"I was wrong to keep you from him ... It wasn't fair to either of you. I was selfish, and I regret that now." She gave my arm a squeeze. "You should go to him ... and tell him who you are ... Tell him you're my son."

"It's too late, now. Too much time has gone by."

"It's never too late to meet your father, Scotty." Her voice trailed off as she turned and looked up at the ceiling. "I'm sorry I never told you sooner."

"You did now. That's all that matters," I assured her and then leaned over to place a kiss on her forehead. "Now, get some rest. It's been a long day."

Just as I was about to walk out of the room, I barely heard her soft voice, "You're a wonderful boy, Scotty. He'll be proud to know you're his."

I wasn't so sure she was right about that. I doubted any man would be exactly thrilled to know that he had a son he never knew about, only to have him show up at his door twenty-one years later. I didn't have a response for her, not one that she'd want to hear, so I just nodded with a half-hearted smile.

"I love you, Scotty."

"Love you, too, Mom."

When I left her room that night, I had no idea that it would be the last time I'd actually speak to her. The next morning, Mom had slipped into a coma and she died two days later. I did my best to be there for Carl, helping him with the funeral arrangements and everything in between, but once the dust had settled, I couldn't handle being in that house—not with all the memories. After I said my goodbyes, I packed a bag and got on my bike, hoping some time on the road would clear my head. A few days later, I found myself in Seattle. In the back of my mind, I think I always knew where I was going. I needed to see him—even if it was just from a distance. It was almost dark by the time I finally found the little brick house with a car and a Harley parked out by the garage. Relieved to see that the lights were on inside, I parked my bike across the street and waited, hoping that someone would eventually come out. Since I hadn't taken the time to search his name or even call the phone number listed on the back of the photograph, I had no idea if he still lived there.

After about an hour of sitting and waiting, the front door finally opened, and a man and a beautiful, young woman stepped outside. The woman rushed to her car, and with a big smile, waved to him and pulled out of the driveway. When I glanced back over to the man, I could tell he was older, much older, but there was no doubt he was the man in the photograph. As he got on his bike, I noticed he was wearing the same leather vest that he'd worn in the photograph. Curious to see where he might be going, I followed him out onto the main drag; after a twenty-minute drive, he turned down an old country road.

When he approached the entrance to an old warehouse, I held back and pulled over on the side of the road and watched as he drove through the gate. I killed my headlight and got off my bike, moving closer to get a better look. There were a bunch of bikes parked by the front door, and every time it opened, I heard loud music blaring from inside. Several guys were standing outside talking with beers in their hand and scantily dressed women at their side. It was right then when I realized my old man was part of a biker club.

One day, after following *my father* for almost two weeks, I went over to the diner across from their garage for a cup of coffee. I was staring out the window, watching the brothers wander in and out of the shop, and never noticed that the front door of the diner had opened. Seconds later, the seat across from me shifted, and I quickly turned to see why, only to get the shock of my life when I found my father staring back at me. "You wanna tell me why the fuck you've been tailing me?"

"What?"

"You don't think I've seen you?" he scoffed. "I know you've been watching me. I just wanna know why."

"I … uh … I," I stuttered, not having a clue what to tell him.

"You got a problem with me, kid?"

"No, sir. I got no problem with you." I certainly didn't want to piss him off. I knew what kind of man he was. Over the past few weeks of stalking him, I'd learned that he wasn't just *part of a club*, he was the fucking president. He'd actually been the one who founded the Chosen Knights. He and a group of his friends started riding together, but it quickly turned into something more. They lived by the motto "Chosen by Fate. Bound by Honor," and it was clear that my old man was pleased with his life and his club.

"You in some kind of trouble with the cops or something?"

I shook my head, "No, sir."

"Then, what the fuck is your deal?"

I didn't want to tell him I was his son, not until he had a chance to get to know me. I wanted to prove myself and show him that I was someone he could be proud of before I told him, so I decided to keep my true identity a secret, at least for the time being. "I was hoping I might be able to prospect for the club."

His eyebrows furrowed. "What makes you think I would let you prospect?"

"I don't know. I guess I was hoping you'd take a chance on me. I've heard a lot of good things about the Chosen and would really like to contribute."

"What the fuck have you got to contribute? The way I see it, you got nothing. I know you ain't got nobody you know around here. No job. No decent place to stay."

"How'd you know that?"

He tugged at his long, unruly beard and chuckled. "Hell, I've had eyes on you since that first night out at the house, boy. You been staying out at the old Weston place, which ain't exactly the nicest dive around"—he glanced down at my cup of coffee and plain piece of toast—"*and* you're running low on cash."

Most of the Chosen's brothers worked blue-collar jobs like mechanics, welders, and line workers. Eventually, they decided to pool their resources and open a shop of their own. Thinking I might be able to use that to my advantage, I said, "Yeah, but I've gotta lot of experience with engines. Almost eight years. There's not a motor I can't fix. New and old. I'm a hard worker, and I think I could be a real asset in your garage."

He sat there listening and studying me as I spoke. I wondered if he might've seen himself when he looked into my eyes. It was doubtful, but maybe, by some kind of intuition, he already knew I was his son. I'm not sure what he saw, but I could definitely tell the wheels were turning inside his head. A man like him wouldn't trust easily, not with the men he's dealt with, but for some reason he seemed to take stock in me. Otherwise, he wouldn't have asked, "You got a name, kid?"

"It's Scotty."

"Okay, Scotty. Are you good at doing what you're told?"

"Yes, sir."

"You know, prospecting isn't for everyone. It's grunt work at its best."

"Yes, sir. I'm good with that. I just need a chance."

He hesitated for a moment, then said, "I'm not making you any promises, but come over to the clubhouse tonight and we'll talk." He stood up and as he gave me a disapproving look, he said, "I'm guessing you still know where it is."

"Yes, sir."

"And kid?"

"Yeah?"

"Stop calling me sir. You're making me feel old as shit." He scowled at me and added, "Just call me Lucky."

I nodded. "Yes, sir."

Shaking his head, he walked towards the door. "See you tonight, kid."

That conversation changed the direction of my life in

ways I couldn't begin to imagine. I got to prospect for my old man and learned that not only was he a good man, loyal and hard-working, but I also discovered that he had a daughter—my half-sister, Zoe. I'd found what I was looking for, and I busted my ass to prove myself to the brothers and to my father. Almost a year had passed, and I'd yet to reveal my identity to my father. I tried to tell him, but the timing was never right. And with each new day, it became harder to come clean about who I really was to him. Now, I'd never get that chance. A few weeks before I was to be patched in, my father wrecked his bike, killing him on impact.

Nothing haunts a person more than the words we'd never get a chance to say. They fester and grow into something they weren't intended to be—lies and untold truths.

Zoe was devastated. Hell, I was, too. It seemed everything I'd worked for was in vain. Without my old man around, things quickly started going to shit in the club; I was actually relieved that no one knew who I was. I considered leaving, but deep down I knew I couldn't walk away from Zoe. Whether she realized it or not, she was family, and it was up to me to protect her. I had no idea how bad things would get after I'd made my decision to stick around, but I saw things that made my blood run cold and knew I had to get Zoe the hell out of there, especially when one of the brothers started making claims to her. Slider was a member of the Chosen with nothing but greed running through his veins—a piece of shit through and through. There was little I could do since I hadn't been patched in yet, but I couldn't have been more relieved after finding out she'd gotten herself tangled up with one of the brothers from Satan's Fury.

When they caught wind of what the Chosen were up to, and that Zoe was in danger, the Fury took them down. By the time they were done, there wasn't a trace of their club or any of their shit left behind. Zoe was finally free, and for that matter, so was I. Once the dust settled, I laid it all out there and told Zoe everything, and when it was all said and done, we'd both found ourselves at the footsteps of the Satan's Fury clubhouse.

DIESEL

One Year Later

LOYALTY. Code. Brotherhood. For the longest time, those were all just words to me. When I made the mistake of prospecting for the Chosen, I threw myself into a world of treachery, betrayal, and death, just so I could try and prove myself to a man who didn't even know I was his son. It wasn't until I spent a year prospecting for the brothers of Satan's Fury when I started to understand what it meant to belong to something that was bigger than yourself. It wasn't easy. Hell, it was one of the hardest things I'd ever done, draining me emotionally, physically, and mentally. I was always on the road, going on runs and following orders, but in doing so, I got to know each and every one of them on a different level. They weren't just members of some club; they were brothers. With them, I gained a sense of family, and by the time I got my patch, there wasn't a single one of them who I wouldn't lay my life on the line for, and there was no doubt they'd do the same for me.

I sat in the truck next to Clutch and groaned while I stretched out my legs, knocking them against the side door. "Damn. I hate a fucking cage."

"You and me both, brother, but with this weather, we don't have a choice," Clutch grumbled and kicked up the windshield wipers, trying to clear the snow and ice from the windshield.

We'd just left Topeka, Kansas and were headed down to Memphis, Tennessee; it was a drive we'd taken many times before. A couple of years back, Cotton, the club's president, had worked out a deal with several of the other Satan's Fury's affiliate chapters to broaden the club's distribution. Together, they'd created a pipeline for transporting illegal weapons, which had grown bigger than any of them had expected. As road captain, it was Clutch's job to ensure the safety of the route from Washington to Memphis. In doing so, he had to change up the exchange points with our affiliate chapters in Salt Lake, Denver, Topeka, Oklahoma City and Memphis. Each location had to be off the radar with obscure entrance and exit points, and it was up to Clutch to find them and make sure the pipeline stayed intact.

I had no idea how long we'd been driving when I asked, "How long until we get to Norman?"

"We'll hit the Oklahoma border in about an hour and a half; it's another two hours from there." He looked over to me, and when he noticed the look of agony on my face, he mocked, "I'm guessing with that peanut-sized bladder of yours, you need a break."

"Peanut-sized bladder? Cut me some slack, man. We've been in this damn truck for seven hours, and my fucking ass is killing me."

"I hear ya. Mine, too." Over the past year, Clutch and I have spent a lot of time together. As a prospect, I did lots of traveling with him, and while all the guys were great, there was something about Clutch that was just easy. I enjoyed my new role as his right-hand man. He was level-headed and rarely let anything get to him, which was a good thing when you were dealing with the brothers of Satan's Fury, where opinions were dished out whether you wanted to hear them or not. His ol' lady, Liv, was pregnant and expecting in the next couple of months, so I knew he was eager to get back—meaning we weren't going to make many stops. I was relieved when he looked over at me and said, "We'll pull off at the next exit."

I nodded and stared out the window, praying for an exit to be close. "You wanna grab a bite to eat while we're there."

"Might as well. Then, maybe we can make it to the Wellington exit before we stop for the night."

After a quick pit stop, we stretched our legs and grabbed some food for the road. It started to snow again as soon as we got back on the road, but we still managed to make good time and pulled into Wellington a few hours later. Clutch had a few locations to check, and once he'd found a place he felt would suit our needs for the pipeline, we pulled into the parking lot of a small pizza place right next to our motel. After ordering our food and drinks, I asked Clutch, "You met Liv down in Memphis, right?"

"Yep." He nodded with a proud smile. "Met her at Daisy Mae's."

"Daisy Mae's? Is that a strip club or something?"

He shook his head. "Fuck, no. It's a diner. The club owns it and the apartment upstairs. While I was there, I stayed in the apartment next to hers, and one thing led to another."

"Did you ever consider staying in Memphis?"

"Hell, no. It's a great place to visit, but I wouldn't live there for shit. I know where home is, and it sure as hell ain't in Tennessee."

Even though I've only been a member of the club for a short time, I knew exactly what he meant. I'd found my home, and there was no other place I'd rather be. Turning to look out the window, I noticed that it had finally stopped snowing. We still had a long drive, so I was hoping that it would finally clear up for good. As soon as we finished eating, we walked over to the motel and grabbed a room. After a few hours of sleep, Clutch was up and ready to roll. Relieved I wouldn't be the one driving, I pulled myself out of bed, used the bathroom, threw some clothes on, and started out to the truck.

It was still dark outside when he started up the engine, but it was clear that Clutch was eager to get going. "Do you need anything before we get out on the road?"

"Is this your way of saying that we're not stopping until we get to Memphis?"

He gave me a small shrug. "It's only six hours, brother. No sense in wasting time."

"Just need a cup of coffee, and I'll be set."

"You can grab one when we hit the gas station up the road."

The minute Clutch pulled up to the gas pump, I jumped out and went inside to get us both some much-needed coffee and a bite to eat; by the time I walked out the door, he was back inside the truck waiting for me. As soon as I got settled, he pulled out onto the main road, and we were on our way to Memphis. Clutch was one of those quiet drivers, spending his time focusing on the road or inside his own head, so I spent the first two hours dozing in and out. By the time we hit Arkansas, I was getting pretty restless; my thoughts turned to meeting the brothers from the Memphis chapter, when I realized I didn't know a lot about them. Hoping to get a better insight to the men I was about to meet, I turned to Clutch and asked, "So, Gus ... he's the president, right?"

"Yeah. He's a good guy. Reminds me of Cotton. Runs his club with honor, even with all the bullshit that goes on in that town. I also got to know Blaze pretty well when I was working at the shop. The guy works his ass off to keep the place running right. He's got a kid named Kevin, who he's raising on his own. His wife died a few years ago, which makes it hard, since his kid's been sick."

"What's wrong with him?"

"He had some kind of cancer, but he's been in remission for a while now. I think Blaze is worried that it might come back," he explained.

"That's gotta be tough."

"No doubt, but he's doing the best he can. I've kept in touch with him, and the last I heard, they were doing alright." I could hear the concern in his voice as he spoke, which made me wonder if he was worried about him getting sick again.

"And the others?"

"I really didn't get to spend a lot of time with many of them." He thought for a moment, then continued, "There's Cyrus. He runs the diner, and he helped me and Liv out when that asshole, Daniel Perry, came looking for them. I'm not sure if you heard about that nightmare. Perry's father and Olivia's were real estate business partners. In order to fuck up a huge development project, that greedy douchebag, Daniel, killed her folks and was planning on doing the same to Liv and her younger brother and sister, thinking he'd get rid of any witnesses. That didn't work out too well for him." He sighed with a disgusted look on his face. "So, I owe Cyrus a lot."

"I see that, and I'm looking forward to meeting them. So, what's the plan when we get there?"

"I'll meet with Gus and go over the changes with the route. I figure we'll crash there tonight. I want to check in with Blaze and Sam and see how they're doing. We can head back in the morning."

"Sam?"

"Sam ... well, that's a long story," he scoffed.

"All I've got is time, brother. Let's hear it." Clutch spent the next half hour telling me how Liv met Sam at the diner. At the time, he was a homeless vet, and she had a soft spot for the old guy. Turned out that he had one for her, too, and he'd been keeping an eye on her and the kids, helping them stay safe during that whole fiasco. Not too long afterwards, the club took him in as a prospect, and now he's a patched member. "Damn. It's a good thing he was around when that asshole came looking for them."

"Yeah, there's no telling what would've happened if he hadn't been there."

We continued talking for the next few hours, which

made the long ride much more bearable. By the time we pulled up to the clubhouse gate, Clutch had told me everything about his time in Memphis, and I felt more prepared to meet the brothers. He rolled down his window when he saw one of the prospects heading over to us. "Clutch and Diesel. We're here to see Gus."

He gave us a quick nod and motioned us on through. Clutch pulled up to the front door and parked the truck. I followed him inside, and as soon as we stepped through the door, someone called out, "Clutch! How's it going, man?"

"Hey, Murph," Clutch answered as he started walking towards one of the brothers with long, shaggy hair and a scruffy beard. Clutch gave him a quick side hug and a slap on the back as he said, "Good to see ya, brother."

"We weren't expecting you until later this afternoon."

"Made good time." Clutch smiled proudly. "I don't reckon you've met Diesel. He's one of our newest members."

Murph extended his hand as he replied, "Good to meet, Diesel. Did you have a good trip?"

"It was alright, but damn, the snow was really coming down at times."

"Heard it's pretty bad up north."

"Yeah. It's a hell of a mess, but it cleared up once we got out of Oklahoma," Clutch replied.

"Hope that shit doesn't make its way down here. People around here lose their mind with just an inch. I can't imagine what they'd do with a foot of snow."

"I think you're safe for now." Clutch chuckled. "Hey, is Gus around?"

"Yeah. He's in his office." Murph turned and called out

to one of the guys at the bar. "Hey, Runt. Clutch is here to see Gus. You mind taking him back?"

He stood up and started walking over to us. "Clutch. Good to see ya, brother."

"You, too, Runt." After he shook hands with him, Clutch turned towards me and said, "I shouldn't be long."

"Take your time," Murph told him. "We'll be waiting for you in the bar."

Clutch nodded, then followed Runt down the hall. Once he was gone, Murph led me into the bar. When we walked in, the place was deserted, so I assumed most of their guys were like us and worked during the day. Murph grabbed us a couple of beers, and as he offered me one, he sat down behind the counter. He didn't look like your typical Sergeant of Arms, but there was a fierceness behind his eyes that let me know he wasn't a man you'd want to get tangled up with. He ran his hand over his beard as he said, "Clutch mentioned that you were new to the club."

"I am." I took a drink of my beer before I said, "Got my patch about a month ago."

"I've only been around him a couple of times, but from what I could tell, Cotton is one of the good ones."

"He is. Proud to be a part of his club," I told him truthfully. "Some of the best men I know."

We spent the next hour talking about anything from reconstructing engines to football playoffs, and just as we were finishing our beer, a hot little number came up behind Murph and slipped her arm around his waist. She leaned towards him, whispering something in his ear, and as he listened, a smirk crossed his face. Once she was done, he looked back at her and said, "Not now, darlin'. We've got company."

After his rejection, she turned her attention to me. As her eyes slowly roamed over my cut, a sexy smile spread across her face. "And who is this handsome fella?"

"This here is Diesel. One of our boys from up North."

"Hi there, Diesel. I'm Jasmine." In a seductive tone, she continued, "It's really nice to meet you."

"Nice to meet you, too."

"Can I get you both another beer?"

"Get us a couple out of the back cooler. Need to restock the one behind the bar," Murph answered.

"Sure thing, babe."

Once she was gone, I looked over to Murph and asked, "She your ol' lady?"

"Hell, no. Jasmine is one of the hang-arounds. Sweet girl, but just like all the chicks around here, she's too young and naïve for me."

Surprised by his response, I said, "So, I take it you don't have an ol' lady."

He shrugged. "Hard to find a woman strong enough to tame the beast."

"Gotcha." I laughed. "It can be a struggle."

Before he could respond, Clutch walked in with an older guy sporting a thick, gray beard following behind. Murph looked over to them and asked, "What about it, Prez? Did y'all get the new drop-off points worked out?"

"We did."

Clutch added, "A couple are a little out of the way, but it's better to be safe than sorry."

"You got that right," Gus answered. "You chose well. Cotton was right to put it in your hands."

"Thanks, Gus. Appreciate that," Clutch replied.

"When's the next run?"

"In just over two weeks. If we ..."

His voice trailed off when Jasmine walked back into the bar. As she placed our beers on the counter, she looked over to me and asked, "Will you be staying at the club tonight?"

"Sorry, darlin'," a man's voice replied. "They've decided to stay over at Daisy Mae's tonight."

Clutch looked over to Gus, and with his hand extended out to him, he said, "Thanks for giving us a place to crash, Gus. I could use a decent meal and a good night's sleep."

"I'm sure you can after that long-assed drive. I'll give Cyrus a call and let him know you'll be heading over."

"Tell him it'll be a bit. I thought I'd run by the garage and see Blaze before we head over."

Gus nodded. "I'm sure he'd be glad to see you, and Sam, too. He's been helping out, and turns out, he's a damn good mechanic."

"Glad to hear that," Clutch replied. "It'll be good to catch up."

"Be careful heading back tomorrow, and let Cotton know I'll be calling him."

As we started towards the door, Jasmine came over to me and said, "Bye, handsome. If you're ever back in town, be sure to come by. I'd love the chance to get to know you better."

"I'll keep that in mind," I told her with a smile.

I followed Clutch outside, and my stomach started to growl as we headed towards the truck. "You said Daisy Mae's had good burgers, right?"

"Best around," he answered as he got inside the truck and closed the door.

"Any chance we'll be going by there any time soon?"

"Soon enough," he mocked. "Trust me. It will be worth the wait."

ELLIE

I had two choices. I could face my fear and risk losing everything, including my life, or I could run. Maybe if I'd had more time to think about the consequences, I would've chosen differently, but instead, I did the only thing I thought I could. With only the clothes on my back and a few bucks in my wallet, I ran. Consumed with panic, my legs didn't feel like my own as I rushed out to my car and got inside, locking the doors behind me. It was as if I was watching a horror movie play out in slow motion, and as much as I wanted to make it all stop, I couldn't. With my hand trembling, I placed the keys in the ignition and started the car. In my entire life, I couldn't remember ever being so scared, and the thought that it was just the beginning only made it worse—if that was even possible. As it was, I couldn't breathe, like someone had their fingers wrapped around my throat, choking me with all their might, and I feared I might faint. Trying to calm my racing heart, I inhaled a slow, strained breath but nothing helped. I just wanted to pull the car over, curl up into a ball, and wait for someone to come save me. But no one would come. I was alone—completely and utterly alone.

I hadn't been driving long when it started to snow again. Since the roads were already covered in ice, it was difficult to keep my car from sliding off the road, but I wasn't taking my foot off the gas for a little snow. I'd just made it into town when I saw a car coming in my direction. I suddenly had an urge to call out to them, to plead for them to help me, but I knew that wasn't an option. I wasn't the person everyone thought I was. So many lies had been told, mountains and mountains of lies, and no one would believe that I wasn't the happy, little homemaker I'd always pretended to be. As I pressed my foot against the accelerator, I glanced up at my rearview mirror, praying that no one was following me. To my relief, there was only darkness behind me.

After an hour of being on the road, I started to settle into the drive, and I found myself thinking back on a time when things were different—a time when I had a family I could turn to, a mother and father who loved me, a brother who always had my back, and friends I could actually trust.

My mother was standing at the kitchen stove with her curly, dark hair and a bright smile on her face, and I could almost hear the comforting sound of her voice as she turned to me and asked, "How was your day, sweetheart?"

I was fifteen years old, and I'd just come home from school. We didn't have a big, fancy house, but it was a place we were proud of. It was home. With mom waiting for my response, I sat down at the table with a soda and a handful of crackers. I gave her a heavy sigh, then said, "It was going pretty good until Maddie and I got into a big argument at lunch."

She turned to face me and leaned against the stove as she crossed her arms. "Argument? About what?"

"Honestly, I don't even know. She was asking me what she should wear on her date with Jason on Friday night, and then she started telling me I should go out with his best friend, Brady. I don't like Brady ... like not at all, and when I told her that, she got mad about it."

From the time Maddie and I had met in pre-school, we were inseparable. When I wasn't at her house, she was at mine. Mom always said that she was like her second daughter, so she simply offered, "Maybe you should try talking to her about it."

"I tried, but she won't listen." I took a sip of my drink, then continued, "She is so wrapped up in Jason that she thinks everything about him is *so wonderful*, including all his knucklehead friends."

"It's her first boyfriend, Ellie. Just be patient with her and try not to be too judgmental of him or his friends." She gave me one of her looks and added, "I'm sure you can find something good about him."

"Jason is a douchebag, Mom."

"Ellie! Young ladies shouldn't talk like that."

Just as she'd gotten the words out of her mouth, my father walked in. He was covered from head to toe with dirt, and from the expression on his face, I could tell he'd had a rough day. "What's going on in here?"

Mom shook her head as she said, "Your daughter is sounding more and more like her brother every day."

"That's not necessarily a bad thing." Dad teased.

"Joseph has a good head on his shoulders, just like his father."

"His father doesn't say the word douchebag, does he?"

"That depends."

"Thomas!" Mom scolded.

Dad turned to me and said, "Ellie, you know better than to talk like that."

"I know. I'm sorry."

He kicked off his muddy boots and lowered his overalls, leaving his dirty clothes in a pile by the back door like he always did, and then, he sauntered over to Mom at the stove. He wrapped his arms around her and kissed her on the cheek. "What's for dinner?"

It seemed like my parents were always touching one another. They were high school sweethearts, and it gave me hope to know that they were still in love after being together for so many years. Mom looked over to him with affection in her eyes as she replied, "Stew and cornbread."

"Sounds good. You know how I love your stew. I'll go take a shower." On his way out, he shouted, "I hope you added lots of potatoes this time."

"I added plenty. I promise."

By the time my father had showered and changed, my older brother, Joseph, had made it home from football practice. We all gathered around the table for dinner and shared our day with each other as we ate. Joseph and I cleared off the table, and while I was at the sink washing dishes, he came over to me and asked, "What happened with you and Maddie today?"

"You heard about that?"

"Jason was bitching about it at practice. Said Maddie was all torn up about it."

"Really?" I asked.

"Yeah. So, what were you arguing about?"

I sighed. "She wants me to go out with Brady."

"Brady? That guy's a real asshole," he grumbled as he put several dirty glasses in my dishwater. "Why would she want you to go out with him?"

Brady was a senior, and while I didn't know him very well, I knew enough to know he wasn't the guy for me. He was a linebacker on the football team, big and burly, and while he was good-looking, he was arrogant as hell. Since he played football, Joseph knew exactly how he was, so I had no doubt that he'd understand my reservations about going out with him. "He's friends with Jason. She wanted us to double date or something. I told her that I didn't want to go out with him, and she got all pissed about it."

"That doesn't make any sense."

"I know. I don't know why she got all worked up about it. It's not like her."

"Well, there's probably something else going on." Like most brothers and sisters, we spent a lot of time arguing, but Joseph was a good brother. I loved him dearly and looked up to him. Whenever he gave me advice, I did my best to listen, but this time I wasn't so sure he was right when he suggested, "You should talk to her. Give her a call, and sort it out."

"But, she's the—"

"Call her, El," he interrupted. "She's your best friend. Don't let this argument fester into something more than it already is."

I took my brother's advice, and as soon as we were done cleaning the kitchen, I went up to my room and called her. It took some time, but I finally got her to tell me what was really bothering her. Apparently, Jason was pushing her to take that next step, but she wasn't ready to sleep with him. She'd hoped that if I was there with Brady, she'd be able to put him off a little longer. After hearing why she was so upset, I agreed to go on the date, and our argument was over. Like always, my brother was right. My best friend needed me, and without his push, I would've never known it.

As I continued to drive down the highway, my mind wandered to a memory that wasn't exactly pleasant. After our double date with Maddie and Jason, Brady and I started dating, and to my surprise, I actually fell for him. I liked him—a lot. He was funny, and he made me laugh. I enjoyed being with him, but there was just one problem. We argued, about *everything*. At first, it was over little things, and we'd just end up laughing it off. But after Brady graduated and went off to school, our little tiffs turned into something more. He became controlling and didn't want me going anywhere without him. At the time, it didn't bother me. I would've rather been with him than anyone else anyway, but when my family figured out what was going on, they wanted me to steer clear of him, warning me that things would only get worse.

Maybe it was just my age or maybe my hormones were corrupting my brain cells, because in my mind, I knew him better than they did. My relationship with Brady caused a big rift between us all, and it only got worse when I got pregnant. I can still remember the argument we had on the front porch of my home. My father's face was red with anger as he growled, "There's no way in hell you're quitting college, Ellie. That's not an option."

"Brady wants me to move in with him. He starts the

academy next week, and by summer, he'll be a police officer. It's going to be okay."

"No. It's not." My mother shook her head. "You're so naïve. Do you honestly think this boy is going to be able to take care of you and your baby on what a police officer makes? You need to finish school. It's the only chance you have."

"I can't go to school and take care of a baby. It's too much."

"You should've thought about that before you spread your legs for that asshole," Dad barked.

"I love him!"

"You're a child! You don't know what love is!"

"*Thomas*. We need to stay calm," she scolded. After a deep sigh, she turned to me and said, "We can help you with the baby while you're at school, and you could always *consider* adoption. You're so young, Ellie. You have your whole life ahead of you ... And this boy, Ellie, he's not the one for you. Deep down, I think you know that."

"I'm not giving up the baby!"

"Okay. Then let us help you. You don't have to move in with him. You can stay here, finish your classes, and we can do—"

"Don't waste your breath, Margret. Look at her." With a disgusted face, he motioned his hand in my direction. "She's already made up her mind. She's not listening to a damn thing we say."

"Because you aren't *listening to me!*" I replied. "I know you don't like Brady, but I love him, and I'm not giving up this baby!"

He took a step towards me as he growled, "Well, listen to this. If you leave and move in with this boy, then you're on your own. It will be your decision, and you'll have to live with the consequences. Don't come crawling back to us when everything goes to hell."

I was surprised by his reaction, but the look on his face told me he meant every word. "Dad, please don't do this. Don't make me choose between you and him."

"It shouldn't be a hard decision. We've never failed to be here for you when you needed us. Can you say the same for him?"

"That's not fair."

"Of course it is, Ellie. So, what's it going to be? Are you going to do the right thing? Are you going to stay here with us and let us help you get through all this, or are you going to walk away?"

Thinking back on my past made me realize that family was so important—it was everything. I had it made. I lived in a nice town with a family who loved me, and then I screwed it all up when I chose Brady over them. If I could go back in time and take it all back, I would. I would do it in a heartbeat, but that's the thing about the past: There's nothing in the world you can do to change it. If I could just go back, I would've stayed there with my mom and dad that day. I would've let them help me and let the cards fall where they may. If I had, I might've actually had the baby, graduated from college, and had the life I'd always dreamed of. Unfortunately, none of that happened, and to make matters worse, I no longer had my family for support. There was no way I would've gone to them now anyway; I couldn't pull them into my nightmare. Not that it mattered anymore, but I had to figure this out on my own.

With the snow falling even harder than before, I just

kept driving. I had no idea where I was going. I just knew I had get as far away from Ellensburg as possible, so I headed into the mountains and prayed that I'd end up somewhere safe. Several hours later, I was running low on gas, and the roads were getting worse by the minute. My eyelids were becoming heavy and my entire body was weak from exhaustion. Even though I needed to find somewhere to stop, I just kept pushing forward. I didn't have a choice. I had no idea where I was, and there were no gas stations, restaurants, or even a house, anywhere in sight. The longer I drove, the harder it was to keep my eyes open, and the minute I closed them, I lost control of my car. It happened in an instant. I felt like I was floating through the air as the car slid towards the edge of the road. Overcome with panic, I tried slamming on the brakes, but it did nothing to stop me from heading towards the embankment. With a terrifying jolt, the car rocked to its side and started to flip—over and over again. I barely had time to scream before the air bags knocked me back and my head slammed against the driver's side window. The sound of breaking glass and crumbling metal was deafening as the car continued to tumble down a long, deep ravine. The whole thing happened in slow motion and seemed to last a lifetime before it all stopped. The car eventually slammed into a thick of trees, leaving me surrounded by silence.

DIESEL

*W*hen we pulled up to Lou's Restoration, there were several old cars parked out front, and even more inside. Where we had the construction company and the dock, they used the garage and the diner to launder their money; from the looks of it, they were doing pretty fucking well. I followed Clutch as he sauntered forward, passing several guys who were busy working, each one of them calling out to him to welcome him back. He'd return their greeting, but he didn't stop. Just as he was about to open the door to the office, it flew open and we were met by a blond-haired guy with an unruly beard and a wide smile. He stepped forward and gave Clutch a quick, firm hug as he said, "Clutch! My man. How's it going?"

"Hey, Blaze. Good to see you, brother," he told him as he patted him on the shoulder.

Blaze turned and went back into the office and asked, "How was the trip down?"

"Not too bad, if you like driving in a fucking blizzard."

Clutch motioned towards me as he followed him into the office. "I don't think you've met Diesel."

I extended my hand to him. "Nice to meet you, brother."

Blaze shook my hand and smiled. "Good to meet you, Diesel."

Once we all sat down, Clutch said, "Looks like things are going good here at the shop."

"They are. Things have really picked up over the last few months."

"What about Duggar? Is he back to work?" Clutch asked.

"Yeah, but after the wreck, he hasn't been able to do as much as he used to. His leg gives him all kinds of trouble, so he's taken a step down and left all the fun stuff to me," Blaze grumbled. "Running the show isn't all it's cracked up to be."

"Yeah, that's what I've heard." Clutch chuckled. "But from what I can see, you're doing pretty well with it. You've got them lined up outside."

Blaze ran his hand through his thick hair as he groaned, "Maybe so, but it doesn't leave me much time for anything else, especially with Kevin. He needs me to be around, and I wanna be with him as much as I can, especially with everything that's been going on with him. It just makes it tough to balance everything out."

I could see the concern in Clutch's eyes as he asked, "How's he doing these days?"

"He's gonna be eight in a few months. He's growing like a damn weed. Hell, I can't keep the kid in shoes. He grows out of them in just a few months, and he's smart. Hell of a lot smarter than I was at his age, especially with those damn electronics. There's nothing that kid can't do, and he likes to rub it in my face whenever he can."

"Eight? Damn. I bet he's a handful."

Blaze smiled. "Yeah, but he's a good kid. Makes me proud every damn day."

"Is he doing okay ... health wise?"

"Yeah. He's still in remission, and the doctors are hopeful he'll stay that way. He seems to be doing okay, although, I can't help but worry. He's all I got, you know, and I don't want to lose him."

Hearing them talk made me think back to when we first found out that my mother had breast cancer. By the time she was diagnosed, it was too late. The doctors suggested several different experimental drugs, but she quickly realized that the side effects were worse than the actual cancer. The disease took its toll on her, making her death long and drawn out. No one should have to go through that, especially a child, and I hoped for Blaze's sake that his son remained in remission. I was pulled from my thoughts when I heard Blaze ask, "Sam told me that Liv was expecting. Congratulations, brother."

"Thanks. I'm still trying to get used to the idea. I can't believe I'm gonna be a father," Clutch replied proudly.

"It'll be the best thing you've ever done. Any idea what she's having?"

"It's a girl. She's due in about eight weeks. We're planning to name her Casey."

"Let's hope she looks like her mother." Blaze teased.

"Don't you know it."

"Well, if she's tall like her father, I bet she'll be one hell of a basketball player."

They continued to talk for another half hour, and then

we headed over to see his buddy, Sam. He was older than I'd imagined, with a long, thick, white beard and deep wrinkles around his eyes. Those eyes lit up when he saw Clutch, and without saying a word, he reached for him and gave him a hug. "It's good to see you, Sam."

His voice was strained as he replied, "I was hoping I'd get to see you while you were in town."

"You know I wouldn't leave without coming by to see you. Liv would have my ass." Clutch teased. "Gus said you've been helping out a lot in the garage."

"I have. It's been good to use my hands again," he explained. "And they need as much help as they can get around here."

"How are things at home? You still staying in touch with your daughter?"

Clutch had told me about Sam having some trouble dealing with his wife's death. He had friends and family who he could turn to, but he just couldn't cope with the loss and ended up living on the streets, doing what he could to escape from the pain. It wasn't something that most would understand, including his daughter, but after everything that happened with Liv, he was able to get his life back on track. I was pleased when I heard him say, "Yep. She's doing good. Met her a fella, and they're talking about getting married."

"That's awesome, Sam. Glad to hear it."

As I stood there watching them talk, it was clear that Clutch was well-liked and had left a highly-regarded impression on the brothers, and they'd equally affected him as well. He'd forged friendships that would last a lifetime, and it made me proud just to witness them all together. Once they were done catching up, Sam gave

Clutch another big hug and wished him and Liv good luck with the baby. We made our way back out to the truck, and Clutch drove us over to Daisy Mae's. As soon as we walked in, I was hit with the smell of home-cooking. At this point I was officially starving, and my mouth started to salivate at the thought of eating a big, thick cheeseburger and fries.

I followed Clutch to the front counter, and we'd barely sat down when I heard, "Clutch. Hey there, brother. It's been awhile."

"Cyrus. It's good to see you, man." Clutch smiled.

He smiled back and heartily shook Clutch's hand. "Gus said you two were going to be staying upstairs tonight."

"That's the plan ... if it's okay with you."

"More than okay, but I got someone staying in the apartment where Liv and the kids stayed, so you two will have to take your old place."

Clutch told me that Cyrus ran the diner with his sister, but that was about it. He was a big guy, covered in tattoos with dark hair and a dark beard to match. There was a look in his eyes that made him seem older, even though he was just a few years older than Clutch.

"That's fine." He looked over to me as he continued, "Diesel here can take the bed. The sofa's more comfortable anyway." Clutch snickered.

Cyrus looked over to me and said, "He's full of shit. Never heard anyone complain about that bed until he came around, and that's only because he's so damn tall his feet hang off the end."

"I'm sure it will be just fine. Hell, I'm so tired I could pass out on the damn floor and sleep like a fucking baby," I told him.

Clutch chuckled then asked, "So, how you been doing?"

"Making it the best I can. You know how Louise can be … always riding my ass about something." He joked. "You'd think she'd eventually wear herself out."

"Nah. Not Louise. She's a tough one, brother."

"You got that right." He rolled his eyes and sighed. "Can I get you two something to eat?"

"Absolutely. How about two sweet teas and a couple of cheeseburgers with fries."

"You got it," he told him as he turned and put in our order. When he came back over with our drinks, he asked, "How are Liv and the kids doing?"

"Doing good. You know, Charlie will be a senior next year."

"Damn. Already?"

"It's hard to believe. And Hadley's growing up fast, brother. Doubt you'd recognize her."

"I don't know, man. She's got a smile that'd be hard to forget."

His cheerful expression quickly changed when a beautiful brunette came walking through the back door. She was a hot little number, around my age and was dressed to the nines with her short, snug-fitting black dress and high heels. Her long, brown hair was down around her shoulders with soft waves that framed her heart-shaped face. She looked over to Cyrus, and her eyes roamed seductively over him like she was about to devour her last meal. When he opened his mouth to speak, she quickly looked away, ignoring him completely as she continued past us. She reached for the handle of the front door and stopped, pausing for a moment like she had something on her mind. I thought she was going to turn around and say something, instead, she suddenly pushed the door open and disappeared into the crowded street.

Once she was gone, Cyrus growled, "Damn."

"Who was that?" I asked.

"No idea. Just know that she's renting the apartment next to your old place."

"You might want to find out more about her ... cause the way she was just looking at you, she either wants to put a bullet in your head or have you for dinner," Clutch taunted.

"Maybe so, but I don't have time for a woman's bullshit right now." He grabbed our burgers from the kitchen window, then slid them over to us. "With everything that's going on with the club, I don't even have a fucking minute to think, so she'll just have to take that shit somewhere else."

"Damn, brother." I snickered. "Things must be rough if you're gonna pass up a chick like that."

"A chick like that is a distraction I don't fucking need, brother."

A concerned look crossed Clutch's face. "Gus didn't mention anything. Is something going on?"

"Same old bullshit. It's bad enough with the fucking gangs in the area, but now we got a new MC sniffing around. We don't need more bullshit," he grumbled. "Just gotta keep these new boys in check and make sure they know what's what."

Clutch took a bite of his burger, then said, "I'm sure Gus will handle them."

"Hell yeah. You know Gus. He don't fuck around. One false move, and he'll string them up by their balls."

"Got no doubt about that. I'd hate to get on his bad side."

"Don't you know it." Cyrus agreed.

Clutch nodded. "And that's why the gavel stays in his hand."

"Damn straight."

We continued to talk as we ate, and an hour later, Clutch and I headed upstairs. It was still early, but we were both wiped from all the traveling. After a hot shower, I collapsed on the bed while Clutch crashed on the sofa. I closed my eyes and listened to the sound of his voice as he talked to Liv on the phone. He asked her a million questions about her day and how she was feeling, leaving no doubt that he was crazy about her. The thought of having kids never really crossed my mind. I'd had a few steady girlfriends in high school, but since then, I rarely dated anyone more than few months. I didn't have the time nor the desire to invest in anything more, but hearing the excitement in Clutch's voice when he talked about the baby had me wondering if I was missing out on something. As soon as he started telling her about his visit with Sam, I finally dozed off.

It felt like I'd just closed my eyes, when Clutch nudged my shoulder and said, "Let's roll."

I turned to face him and yawned. "What time is it?"

"It's time for us to get on the road. Now move your ass," he growled.

Reluctantly, I threw the covers back and pulled myself out of the bed. I padded into the bathroom and did my business, splashed some cold water on my face and brushed my teeth before I got dressed. After I pulled my boots on, I announced, "I'm ready."

"It's about time," he scowled as he started towards the door. Shaking my head, I ignored his irritable mood, grabbed my things, and followed him out to the truck. As soon as we got outside, and my sleeping brain realized that it was still pitch black, I checked my phone to see what time it was. "Fuck, Clutch. It's 4:30 in the damn morning."

"And?"

Knowing he was eager to get back, I grumbled, "Nothing. Let's get home."

"That's what I thought."

As soon as I got in the truck, I glanced over at Clutch and cringed when I noticed the look of determination in his eyes. Damn. I was going to be in for one hell of a ride home.

ELLIE

I was stuck in a dream—a dream I didn't want to be in. I was back in the old apartment that Brady and I moved into right after we'd gotten married. Not only was I trying to adjust to being a newlywed, but I was also dealing with the fatigue and influx of hormones from my pregnancy. I wasn't handling it so well, and Brady wasn't making it any easier. He wanted to follow in his father's footsteps and become a police chief, so he went to the academy. After he graduated, he tried to get a job at our local police department, but he didn't make the cut. He worked hard to prove himself, giving it everything he had, but it just wasn't enough. Since his father was the chief in a neighboring city, he was able to pull a few strings to get him in. Knowing that he hadn't gotten the job on his own changed something in Brady. He became more determined than ever to make a name for himself, but his lack of patience to earn his way up the ladder, along with a derisive attitude towards some of the guys, made him highly unpopular with his colleagues at the precinct.

He quickly became frustrated and angry, and soon developed a habit of stopping off at the bar on his way home. At first, it was just every now and then. He'd drink a few beers, and then he'd come on home. But over time, it became an everyday thing, and to make matters worse, he wasn't the best at handling his alcohol. After spending the night drinking, he would come home and either pass out on the recliner or he'd turn into a raging lunatic, cursing and yelling about everything that was wrong in his life. Unfortunately, the latter happened more often, and I was usually the brunt of all the negative things that were going on.

While I wasn't exactly eager for him to come home that night, I'd fixed dinner and was becoming anxious that he hadn't responded to any of my texts. It was well after dark, so I finally gave up on him and ate dinner without him. Once I was done, I went to the living room to watch TV. I'd just started to doze off when I heard the front door open, and Brady came stumbling into the kitchen. He clambered and banged around for several moments before he finally slammed the door behind him. I sat up on the sofa when I heard him grumble, "Damn it!"

"Brady?" I stood up and walked over to him. "Are you okay?"

His eyes grew narrow as he glared at me with anger. "Not that you fucking care, but yeah. *I'm fine.*"

"I do care, Brady," I told him with sincerity.

"If you cared, you wouldn't be riding me all the time, especially when I'm busting my ass to keep a goddamn roof over your head."

"I was just asking if you were okay," I snapped. "I didn't realize that was *riding you.*"

He took a charging step forward as he spat, "Watch your fucking tone, El! I'm not listening to your bullshit tonight."

Brady had lost his temper many times since we'd moved in together, but I'd never seen him quite so furious. Fearing he might completely lose it, I took a step back. "I'm sorry."

His face grew red as the vein in his neck started to pulse with rage. Spit flung from his bottom lip as he snarled, "You should be sorry, you lazy fucking whore."

"Brady," I mumbled. "You're drunk."

In an instant, he charged towards me with his hand hurtling through the air, and my head lashed back as his palm collided against my face. Before I had a chance to react, he reached for my neck, wrapping his fingers tightly around my throat and slammed me against the wall. "Do you have any idea why I go to the bar every night after work?"

I shook my head frantically as I clawed at his hands. I tried my best to break free, but his grip only tightened, making it impossible to get away from him.

"Because instead of living the life I wanted, I have to come home to you. Every goddamn day I have to see your fucking face, and it makes me sick to my damn stomach. You ... make ... me ... *SICK!*"

The lack of oxygen was making me dizzy, and the room started spinning at my feet. Lights flashed through my eyes, blurring my vision, and my knees became weak. By the time he finally loosened his grip, I was almost unconscious. He gave me a shove, and I lost my footing. I stumbled back, tumbling over one of our kitchen stools, and a thundering bang echoed through the room as it fell to the floor. While I tried to brace myself, there was nothing I could do to stop myself from landing right on top of it. A shooting pain jolted through my side as my gut crashed against the edge of the seat. I cried out, but no sound came from my mouth.

With Brady looming over me, I curled into a ball, wrapping my arms around my stomach in hopes of protecting the baby, but it did little to shield me from his boot as it came crashing into my side. "Now look what you did, you stupid, fucking bitch."

Tears streamed down my face as I clung to my stomach, pleading, "Please stop, Brady. The baby. You're gonna hurt the baby."

It was like someone had flipped a switch, and he suddenly froze. He looked down at me in horror, then knelt beside me. He ran his hand over my head as he mumbled, "Oh, God. What have I done?"

My voice was strained as I told him, "Don't ... touch me."

"Oh, Ellie. I'm so sorry, sweetheart. You know I didn't mean it."

I remained in the fetal position as I demanded, "Get the hell away from me, Brady."

Reluctantly, he stood up, and after picking up the fallen stool, he walked over to his recliner and sat down. The room fell silent as he sat there staring at me on the floor. I was in agony, and the pain only grew more intense as the adrenaline faded from my body. While I laid there on the cold, hard tiles, I tried to steady my breathing, but the cramping was so intense that I had a hard time keeping myself from passing out. Suddenly, I felt a warm sensation between my legs, letting me know something was terribly wrong. I looked down and saw that my thighs were covered in blood.

"Oh, God. No!" I pleaded.

Using all the strength I could muster, I pulled myself up from the floor, and once I was standing, I looked over to Brady. He was passed out in the recliner, and completely oblivious to what was going on. I knew if there was any chance of me saving my baby, I had to get to the hospital. Knowing I couldn't count on Brady, I grabbed my keys and hobbled out to my car. With my hand on my stomach, I drove to the ER, sobbing uncontrollably the entire way. In all my life, I'd never felt such pain—not just physically, but mentally as well. Deep down, I knew that I was going to lose the baby, and the thought of losing her, especially like this, broke my heart. By the time I made it to the back door of the hospital, I was covered in blood. I knew I couldn't walk, so I laid my hand on the horn until one of the orderlies came outside to help me.

With a worried expression, he came rushing over to my window and asked, "What's wrong? Are you okay?"

"No. I'm f-five and a half m-months pregnant, and I'm bleeding r-r-really bad. I th-think I may be having a miscarriage," I stammered from sobbing so hard.

Without hesitation, he opened my car door and took me into his arms, cradling me as he rushed me inside. Moments later, I was on a hospital bed with doctors and nurses hovering over me. I was bombarded with questions that I didn't know how to answer: "Were you in an accident? Were you attacked? Who did this to you?" I remained silent as they continued to examine me, and my worst fears were confirmed during my ultrasound. I heard the doctor tell the nurse that the trauma to my uterus had caused a placental abruption, and there was nothing they could do to save my daughter. Tears trickled down my cheek as I stared up at the ceiling and tried to make sense of everything that was happening. We had our fair share of arguments, but I never dreamed that Brady could be so violent, so cruel. I loved him, or at least I thought I did, but I knew nothing would ever be the same between us again. He'd killed our unborn child, and I would never be able to forgive him for that.

I could hear the torment in the doctor's voice when he said, "I'm so sorry."

"Is she gone?"

"I'm afraid so." He paused for a minute, and then asked, "Is there anyone we can call for you?"

I looked back towards the ceiling as I answered, "No. There's no one."

He placed his hand on my shoulder and gently explained, "Ellie, I'm afraid you're too far along for a D & C. We're going to give you medication to help induce labor—"

"W-wait. What are you saying?"

"You're going to have to deliver the baby. I know it's going to be difficult for you, especially after *whatever* you've gone through tonight, but it's our only choice," he added.

I felt my world come crashing down around me as I was wheeled into the delivery room. While crying hysterically, the nurse put an IV in my arm and started pumping the drugs through my veins. Once she was done, she came over to me and whispered, "I'm here if you need anything."

The delivery was a complete blur. I barely remember any of it. I was too distraught to take in the moment, but once she was born, my world stood still. I watched as the nurse wrapped her in a little, white blanket and brought her over to me. "Would you like to see her?"

In almost a whisper, I answered, "Yes. Please."

The nurse placed my daughter in my arms, and as I looked down at her precious little face, at her rosy, little cheeks and button nose, I'd never felt such love for anything in my life. I circled my fingers across her face and over her perfect little lips, then trailed them down her arm to her hand. Her little fingers were so tiny. Everything about her was tiny, so very tiny, and as I brought my hand back up to her little head, she felt warm to the touch, making it difficult for my mind to accept that she was really gone. I lowered my mouth to her ear as I whispered, "I'm so sorry this happened, my sweet girl. You have to know that I would do anything to take it back. I shouldn't have provoked him. I should've protected you. It was my fault. It was *all my fault.*"

Tears streamed down my face as I kissed her on the forehead, then I nestled her close to my chest and wept. I cried until I had no more tears, and then I cried some more. Losing my daughter broke my heart in a way that I knew it would never be the same again. I couldn't take it anymore. I needed to wake up from this dream. I couldn't stand to watch that nurse take my baby from my arms, not again.

I thrashed my head from side to side and forced myself to wake up. When I finally managed to open my eyes, my bad dream was quickly forgotten. I was in my car with my mangled body pressed against the driver's side door. There was snow trickling through the busted passenger side window, while the others were completely covered in white, making it impossible to see out. I was freezing and could barely feel my fingers as I reached up to touch my throbbing head. My entire forehead was sticky, and my whole face was swollen, including my eyes. Through squinted eyelids, I looked down at my hands and realized they were covered in blood. On further inspection, I saw that it wasn't just my head that was bleeding. I had cuts and scrapes all over my body. I leaned forward to look in the rearview mirror but stopped when a stabbing pain shot through my ribcage. I laid back against the seat and took a strained breath as I tried to make sense of what was happening.

My teeth were chattering from the cold, and I had no idea where in the hell I was. I was bleeding badly, and the freezing temperatures were only making my situation worse. It was then that I'd wished I had my cellphone, but I'd left it behind. I hadn't wanted to take any chances, and it wasn't like there was anyone I could call. Knowing I couldn't just sit there, I unbuckled my seatbelt and tried to pull myself out of my seat. Every muscle in my body burned in searing pain with every move I made, but I was eventually able to pull my feet up to my side and force myself into a standing position. After taking a few deep breaths, I carefully reached into the backseat for my hat and gloves and put them on. I slid on my coat and zipped it up tight, then started out the broken window. The pain was excruciating as I tried to pull myself up through the window, but by the grace of God, I made it. Once my feet were steady on the ground, I glanced up the hill and gasped when I saw how far the car had fallen. My chest tightened when I looked around and all I could see were trees. I was too far down the ravine to even see the road. Everything was covered in white, making it hard to know which direction I should go, but I needed to get out of there alive; I had no choice but to take a chance and move forward and up.

I walked for hours, and with each step, I grew colder and weaker. My ribs were killing me, making each breath strained and painful, and as much as I wanted to stop and take a break, I knew I couldn't. The sun had fallen, and I was surrounded in darkness in the thick of the forest with no sign of life around me, completely exhausted and disoriented. My body was trembling, and with the temperature dropping, I knew I would die if I didn't keep moving. So, I continued my treacherous hike through the forest.

I couldn't see anything as I trudged through the thick snow as there was no moon. Only one tree after the next. Things were looking bleaker by the minute, and I was about to give up hope when I finally noticed a faint light shining in the distance. Maybe it was a mile away, maybe not. I wasn't sure if I could even make it that far, but I knew my only chance of survival was getting to that tiny glimmer of light. My legs felt like lead weights as I forced myself to continue forward, and after what seemed like hours, I was close enough to make out a large building with a tall fence wrapped around it. I could hear the faint sound of music and took that as a sign that someone might be inside. By the time I made it to the fence, my clothes were completely covered in ice and blood, and my entire body was numb. Hanging on by a thread, I clung to the fence and tried to keep my eyelids from falling shut. I was running out of time. I could feel myself becoming dizzy and feared I would pass out before I could make it inside. I held onto the fence as I hobbled forward, using it to help me keep my balance, and eventually made my way around.

Once I'd gotten through the gate, I stumbled, tripping over my own feet and collapsed in the snow.

DIESEL

⁂

*T*he drive time from Memphis, Tennessee to Port Angeles, Washington takes the average man approximately thirty-six hours. Even with the blizzard of a lifetime, Clutch managed to make it back home in just over thirty-four hours. He only made three stops for meals and gas, and one brief siesta at a rest stop outside of Oklahoma. By the time we pulled up to the clubhouse, I was more than ready to get a hot shower and crash. It was just after ten p.m. when we finally got out of the truck and headed inside. Since it was a week night, and most of the guys went home early to be with their families, we both were surprised to find Cotton at the bar talking with Maverick, Stitch, and Smokey. As we started walking towards them, I noticed the expression on Cotton's face and knew immediately something was up. Before I could open my mouth, Clutch asked, "What's going on?"

Cotton looked over to him and said, "That's just it. We don't have a fucking clue."

"It's something you'll just have to see for yourself," Smokey told him as he stood up. "Come on. I'll show you."

We followed him as he started down the hall, and when we got to the med room, he stopped and motioned us inside. Clutch walked in ahead of me, and I could hear the shock in his voice as he said, "What the hell happened to her?"

"Got no idea. Maverick found her passed out in the snow. She's in pretty bad shape."

I walked over to the gurney, and my stomach turned at what I saw. Her head was covered with a large, white bandage, along with her hands. Her eyes were practically swollen shut, and her face was covered in bruises and lacerations. "Fuck man. Why didn't you take her to the hospital?"

Cotton came up behind us and said, "We were going to, but she came to long enough to beg us not to. She was pretty adamant about it. I figure she's running from someone or something and doesn't want to take the chance on being caught. And from what Doc found, I can't blame her."

"What do you mean?"

"Looks like she's had a long run of having the shit beat out of her. She's covered in old scars." He walked over to the side of the bed and added, "It's hard to tell without x-rays, but Doc thinks she's had several broken bones over the past couple of years."

"Any idea where she came from?"

Smokey shook his head. "That's just it. She showed up here with no identification on her. No car. No purse. Nothing. It's like she came out of thin air."

"But she had to come from somewhere," Cotton added.

"Either somebody dropped her off, which means there's no telling who the hell she is, or she managed to get here on her own. Either way, we've got to find out."

"That's kind of hard when she's been out for the past twenty-four hours."

"That long?" I asked. "Damn. Is she going to make it?"

"I don't know. Doc's been working on her since we found her last night, but it's not looking good," Cotton answered.

When Doc came out of the back room, Smokey asked, "How's she doing?"

A somber look crossed his face as he answered, "No change, but that's not necessarily a bad thing. I've given her a pretty strong sedative to help her sleep. Her body needs time to heal, and the rest will do her good."

"What about you? It's about time you had a break."

"I'm good for a few more hours. I don't want to leave her just yet."

"Then, we'll leave you to it. If anything changes, let me know," Cotton told him as he started for the door.

Smokey and Clutch followed him out, but I didn't move. For some unexplainable reason, I felt compelled to stay. I looked down at her, studying the bruises on her face and arms, and I couldn't help but wonder what in the hell happened to her. The clubhouse was miles away from town, surrounded by a thick forest of trees, and with the weather being at its worst, I couldn't imagine how she'd gotten here. Doc walked over to me and said, "I've got no idea who she is, but I do know … that girl has one hell of a will to survive. She was damn near frozen to the bone when they brought her in here, and with all the blood she'd lost, I thought for sure we'd lose her. But she's still hanging on."

"Do you think someone did all this to her?"

"Can't say for sure. There are some strange bruises around her neck. It could be that someone was choking her, but with the large contusion on her forehead, the bruised ribs, and all the other cuts and bruises, it could be that she was in some kind of accident … maybe a car crash. Then, I'd say the bruising could possibly be from a seat belt." He shrugged. "The boys went out looking for some sign of a vehicle off the road but couldn't find anything with all this damn snow."

"If this was an accident, what about the other stuff? Cotton said it looked like she'd been hurt before … that she'd had a rough go of it."

"Yeah. She's got several old injuries and scars. That poor girl has been through hell and back." He ran his hand across his face as he sighed. "I'll tell you one thing … I'd like to get my hands on the asshole who hurt her and show him a thing or two."

I had no idea who this woman was, but watching her fight for her life instilled a sense of rage deep within me. I wanted to take the motherfucker who hurt her and rip him apart, limb by limb. In almost a growl, I replied, "I'd like to have my turn when you're done."

"We've got to find out who we're dealing with first." He patted me on the back and said, "Why don't you go get some rest? I know how it can be riding with Clutch. I'm sure you had a long run of it today. She's not going anywhere. Sleep a few hours, and then maybe you could sit with her while I get a little shut-eye myself."

"Yeah. I can do that."

Again, I found myself not wanting to leave her, and I had to force my feet into motion. I got to the door, and as I stopped to look back over at her, I felt the strangest feeling wash over me. Maybe it was my primal need to protect a helpless female, or maybe it was just seeing that she was so close to death, but I felt an odd pull to her. I tried to shake it off as I headed down the hall. I was exhausted and too tired to drive back to my place, so I decided to just crash in my room at the club. After a hot shower, I laid down on my bed and tried to sleep, but when I closed my eyes, all I could see was her. My mind raced with different possible scenarios of how she'd been hurt and how she'd ended up at the clubhouse. The whole thing was a mystery to me, and my curiosity had me determined to solve it. Sleep finally took over, but it wasn't for long. The sun had just started to filter through the blinds when I found myself wide awake and staring at the ceiling. Knowing there was no way I was going to be able to fall back asleep, I pulled myself out of bed and got dressed. As soon as I got my boots on, I headed straight for the infirmary.

When I walked in, Doc was sitting in a chair next to her bed, and he looked like he was just about to doze off. "How's she doing?"

He stood up and said, "No change. Her stats are good, but she's still out. Hopefully, she'll come around soon."

"You ready for that break?"

"Absolutely. I'm too old for this shit," he groaned. When he got to the door, he turned to me and said, "I'll be in my room. Come get me if anything changes."

"You got it."

I walked over to the bed and was pleased to see that

some of the swelling had gone down. Her eyes were no longer completely swollen shut, and while they were still dry and cracked, the cut on her bottom lip looked like it was starting to heal. It shouldn't have come as a surprise. Doc was one of the best. Before he joined the club, he'd been a doctor in the military, and he's always been there whenever one of the brother's needed him. He could do it all—from your everyday cold and allergies to life-threatening gunshot wounds, and I hoped he'd be able to do the same for her.

I hadn't been there long when Cotton came by. He was followed by Smokey and Maverick, and then Stitch—each of them staying just long enough to see if she was awake. Once they were gone, I stood over her and took a moment to look at her—really look *at her* and not just her battle wounds. Even with the bruising and swelling, I could tell that she was beautiful. She was in her mid-twenties, tall with subtle curves, and her hair was long and dark. As she lay there sleeping, she looked so peaceful, like an angel, and I found myself wanting to know everything about her. I glanced down at her left hand, quickly searching for a wedding ring, and while I found no ring, I could see a faint indentation around her ring finger. Yet another mystery.

For hours, I watched the rise and fall of her chest as I waited for her to wake up, but she never opened her eyes. When I couldn't stand the silence a minute longer, I stepped over to her and gently ran my hand across her cheek as I whispered, "Come on, angel. It's time for you to wake up."

Her skin felt warm to the touch when I placed my hand on her shoulder and gave her a gentle squeeze. "My name's Scotty, but the guys call me Diesel. I know it's an odd name, but that's how it goes when you have one bad go of starting a fire. You get yourself a road name that leaves an impression. Anyway, you're in Port Angeles at the Satan's Fury clubhouse. One of the brothers found you outside in the snow the other night. You were pretty banged up. Bleeding and half frozen. Our guy, Doc, has been working on you, but you gotta do your part. He told me that you're a fighter. I need you to prove it. Open your eyes."

I never took my eyes off her as I continued talking, hoping by some chance that I would be able to convince her to wake up. "You don't have to be afraid. You're safe here. We won't let anyone hurt you ever again. *I* won't let anyone hurt you again. You have my word on that."

I ran my hand down her arm until it reached hers and then placed it in mine. "You can trust me."

I was still holding her hand when I felt her fingers twitch. "That's it, angel. It's okay. You can come back now. I'm here, and I'm not going anywhere."

Her eyelids fluttered as a low groan vibrated through her chest, and after several long seconds, she finally opened her eyes. As her eyes skirted around the room, a look of panic crossed her face and her breath quickened. Knowing she had to be freaked out by her surroundings, I said, "Easy there, doll. You're okay."

She slowly turned her head towards me, and the fear in her eyes was quickly replaced with confusion. Her voice was low and scratchy as she asked, "Who are ... you, and where ... am ... I?"

"I'm Diesel," I told her. "I'll explain the rest later, but first I need to let Doc know you're awake."

When I started towards the door, she reached for me. "Don't ... go."

I placed my hand on top of hers and said, "I'll only be gone a second."

While it was clear from her expression that she didn't want me to leave, she gave me a quick nod. "Okay."

I rushed out the door and then down the hall to get Doc. As soon as I told him she was awake, he shot out of the bed and hurried down to the infirmary. Standing beside her bed, he shined a small light into her eyes and said, "Welcome back. You gave us all quite a scare."

She looked more confused than ever, so I explained, "This is Doc. He's the one who saved your life."

"Saved my life?" She brought her hand up to her head and asked, "What are you talking about? What ... happened?"

"I don't know, darlin'. I was hoping you could answer that," Doc told her.

"I don't know. I ... can't remember."

"That's okay. It'll come to you," he assured her. "What about your name? Do you remember that?"

Her face twisted into a grimace as she tried to think, and after a long pause, she answered, "No. I ... can't remember."

"You've had quite a hard knock to the head. Things will be pretty jumbled up for a little while, but it will sort itself out. Just give it some time."

She glanced back over to me, and with a strained voice, she asked, "What is ... this place?"

"You're at our—"

I started, but Doc interrupted me by saying, "We need to get Cotton and let him know she's awake."

"Can't we wait a minute? Give her a second to come around a bit?"

"You know we can't," he replied. "You go find him while I check her stats."

Before I left, I looked down at her and said, "I'll be right back. You gonna be okay while I'm gone?"

She nodded, and with great hesitation, I headed out to find Cotton. As soon as I told him she was awake, he called Maverick and Stitch, telling them to head over to the infirmary. She was already scared, and when my brothers came barreling into the room, it nearly sent her over the edge. Her face grew pale and her eyes widened with pure terror as she watched them file into the room. Doc patted her on the arm as he said, "Don't you worry now. These men are here to help you."

Cotton approached the side of the bed and asked her the same question Doc had already asked. "Do you got a name, Miss?"

"I can't ... remember."

"You got any idea how you got here?"

She shook her head as she replied, "No. I can't remember ... *anything*."

I knew Cotton wasn't happy with her answers. Like the rest of us, he wanted to know who she was and where the hell she came from, but we'd all just have to wait. In time, she'd answer all of our questions, but her answers would only lead to more questions— questions that would turn her world, and ours, upside down.

ELLIE

*E*very inch of my body was throbbing in pain, especially my head, and I was still trying to break free from the fog that was weighing down on me as I looked around the room. I started to get nervous when I realized it looked less like an actual hospital and more like a room at a veterinarian's office with all the odd cabinets that lined the walls and the peculiar smell that filled the room. It had a strange assortment of medical gear and supplies, and they were far from modern, making the entire room look like something out of the past. I was still trying to become accustomed to my surroundings when they walked into the room. That's when I really started to panic. They were big and fierce with various tattoos marking their skin, and they were each wearing leather vests with skulls and embroidery on the sides and back. As they towered over me and prodded me with questions, it was impossible not to feel intimidated, especially by the man who was standing off to the side. He was tall and muscular with dark hair and a beard, and the way he stared at me with those dark, penetrating eyes chilled me to the bone. I would've been completely freaked out if it hadn't been for *him*—the man who called himself Diesel. The way he spoke to me in that deep, calming voice, and how he looked at me with those kind, green eyes, made me feel less threatened—like I was safe in this crazy place I'd found myself in.

An older man with salt-and-pepper hair and a goatee hovered over me as he asked, "What exactly do you remember?"

My mind was still trying to fight the fog I was under, and every memory seemed so far away, unable to be reached. I wanted to answer his question, but I didn't know how, and that terrified me even more. "I don't know. I can't explain it. I don't remember anything. I don't know how I got here. I don't know how I was hurt. I don't even know my name. How can this be happening?"

Doc came over to me with compassion in his eyes as he said, "She's just now coming around. We need to give her some time, Cotton."

"I'll give you some time," he told me as he glared at me with suspicion. "But if you're hiding something, it's only going to make it worse. If there is something going on, I need to know about it. I don't like *surprises*."

"I wish I could tell you ... but I can't remember anything."

"Well, if that changes, I want to be the first know," he demanded.

Doc looked over to him and nodded. As they started to file out of the room, Cotton stopped and looked back over to me. In a deep, authoritative voice, he commanded, "I want someone with her at all times. She isn't to be left alone ... Understood?"

Diesel answered, "With the weather the way it is, things are slow at the construction site and in the garage, so if it's good with you, I can stay with her. Doc and I will let you know if there's any change."

"Sounds good to me."

Relief washed over me as I watched them walk out of the room. Doc and Diesel talked quietly between themselves for a moment, and for the first time, I finally got a good look at Diesel. He was wearing loose fit jeans that were frayed at the hem and a long-sleeve, black t-shirt, which brought out the olive tone in his skin. Although he wasn't as big as the others, he was still very muscular and tall. While I was checking him out, Doc came over to me and asked, "Are you up for eating something?"

I was caught off guard by the question, so it took me a minute to answer. "Umm ... No. Not really."

"We've got to get something in your system, darlin'. Even if it's just a piece of toast or something."

The thought of eating just didn't appeal to me, but I knew he was right. "Okay. Maybe some toast?"

"You got it. I'll be back in a few minutes. Diesel is going to stay with you. If you need anything, just let him know."

"Um ... Before you go ... I really need to go to the bathroom," I whispered.

"I can help with that." He walked over to Diesel and motioned for him to step outside. Once he was gone, he pulled my blankets back, and I was surprised to see that I was only wearing my bra and panties. When he noticed my expression, he said, "Your clothes were wet and covered in blood. We'll get you something to wear in just a bit."

"Oh."

He helped me to my feet, and as soon as I tried to stand, I found that my legs were like noodles, and I stumbled forward. Before I dropped to the floor, he reached for me, pulling me to his side as he helped me walk towards the bathroom. Once I was on the inside, I eased the door closed and stepped over to the mirror. I gasped with horror when I saw my reflection. I looked like I had been in some kind of battle, and I'd lost miserably. As I held onto the sink for balance, I stared at my reflection for several moments, trying to force myself to remember what had happened to me, but no memories came. When my legs started to tremble, I finally gave up, went to the bathroom, and walked back out to Doc. As he helped me back over to the bed, I told him, "I don't know why you did it, but thank you for saving my life."

"No need to thank me. Just trying to do what's right." He patted me on the leg. "Now, get some rest. I'll grab you something to eat and some clothes. Are you going to be alright here with Diesel?"

"Yes, I think so."

He walked over to the door and once he opened it, he motioned for Diesel to come back inside. They spoke for a moment, then Doc walked out into the hall, leaving us alone. Diesel came over and asked, "You doing okay?"

"I would be doing better if you would tell me where I am and who those men were."

"You're at the Satan's Fury clubhouse."

"Satan's Fury? What are you talking about?"

"Satan's Fury is a motorcycle club. Have you heard of 'em?" he asked.

"I've heard of motorcycle clubs before, but I've never heard of Satan's Fury. Should I be worried about these guys?"

"I'm one of 'these guys,' and you're alive, aren't ya? You've gotta remember ... these are the people who are trying to help you. They gave you a roof over your head with a warm bed, medical attention, and whatever else you may need. I'd say you already have the answer to that question."

"You're right, and I really do appreciate it. But there's just so much that I don't know ... like ... how did I end up here?"

"That's just the thing." He shrugged. "None of us know. The clubhouse is miles away from town. Got nothing out here but trees and mountains. It's like you showed up in the middle of thin air. And on top of that, when Maverick found you out there in the snow, you had no car, no identification, and you were just about dead when they brought you in here. You'd lost a lot of blood ... had a pretty nasty bump on your head, severely bruised ribs, and scratches and cuts all over. It's a miracle Doc was able to bring you back."

"How is that possible? I had to come from somewhere."

"You're right about that, and in time, we'll figure it out." Even with a storm of confusion raging inside me, there was something about the way he spoke that set me at ease. I couldn't explain it, but I knew I could trust him. "For now, you just need to get some rest and try to get better."

Moments later, Doc returned. "I got you some things to wear and a bite to eat as well."

"Thanks, Doc," I told him as I took the folded clothes from his hands.

As Diesel started towards the door, he said, "I'll step outside while Doc helps you get dressed."

I was able to put on the black knit leggings without any trouble, but the long-sleeved t-shirt was a different matter. With my aching ribs, I couldn't manage it on my own. Seeing my struggle, Doc came over to me and took the shirt from my hand, careful not to hurt my wound as he eased it over my head and helped me slip my arm through each of the sleeves. Once that was done, he checked my bandages and gave me some medicine for the pain. Even though I wasn't hungry, I managed to eat a few bites of toast and drank a little tea, which seemed to satisfy Doc, at least for the time being. "I've gotta run home and check on a few things. When I get back, we'll see about getting you moved to a more comfortable room."

"That's okay. I'm fine here."

"No. A room like this isn't suitable for a young lady like yourself." He reached for his coat and as he put it on, he added, "You need anything, just let Diesel know and he'll take care of it."

"I'm sure I'll be fine."

He gave me a quick nod, and then started for the door. Once he stepped outside, Diesel walked back in. As he came over and sat down next to me, he asked, "You feeling better?"

"Yes, but I'd be feeling even better if I could remember something ... *anything*. I just don't understand it." Something occurred to me as I thought about everything that had happened. "Can I ask you something?"

"Sure."

"If I was in such bad shape, why didn't you just take me to the hospital?"

He shrugged. "They were going to, but just before you passed out, you begged them not to. Cotton figured there had to be a reason why, so he got Doc to fix you up."

"Why wouldn't I want to go to the hospital?"

"I don't know, but there had to be a good reason. Probably had something to do with why you were out in the middle of snow storm." His eyes dropped to the floor like he was thinking about something. After several seconds, he looked back to me and asked, "I know you can't remember your name or what happened, but is there anything you *can remember*?"

I closed my eyes for a moment, and as I tried to think back, I was bombarded with images of people's faces, a house with a front porch, a kitchen, an apartment, and all the sounds of voices, but they were all jumbled up. I couldn't make sense out of any of it. "It's like all these memories are right there … I can almost reach them, but they're just too far away. Does that make any sense?"

"It does, and they will come to you when you're ready. It's just going to take some time."

My voice trembled as I asked, "Are you sure? What if my memory never comes back?"

"You've got to take this thing one step at a time, angel. It'll all sort itself out. Just give it a little time and don't push yourself. You'll see."

"Why are you being so nice to me? You don't even

know me. I could be a horrible person. I could've done something terrible. What if that's the reason I'm here."

"Maybe you did do something bad. Hell, if I know, but somehow, I doubt it. I've always been pretty good at reading people, and you don't seem like the kind of person who could've done something all that bad. So, the way I see it, we just have to wait and see how the cards fall."

"Can I ask you how you got the name *Diesel*? Is that really your name, or is it a nickname or something?"

"My real name is Scotty. Diesel is my road name. I acquired it after I had a little mishap with some fuel and starting a fire. Over time it just stuck, and the brothers have been calling me Diesel ever since."

"What do you mean ... *brothers?*"

"It might be hard for you to understand, but we're all family here. The guys here are my brothers, and there's nothing I wouldn't do for them ... *nothing.*"

"But they're not really your family, right?"

"Not by blood. They're my family *by choice.*"

"I think I understand ... Well, maybe I do." I smiled. "I always thought clubs like these were just an excuse for guys to get together and drink, and when the weather's nice, they'd ride their bikes."

"That's how it is for some, but we tend to take things a little more seriously around here," he explained.

"I can tell," I scoffed. "I thought that Cotton guy was going to blow a gasket when I told him I couldn't remember who I was."

His friendly tone quickly changed as he said, "Cotton's our president. It's his job to keep things running around here, and for all any of us know, you could be something other than what you say you are."

"Considering how I got here, who else could I be?"

"Considering how you just showed up ... out of the fucking blue, with no car and no ID ... you could be *anyone*."

"And that's why that Cotton guy doesn't want me to be left alone?"

"Exactly."

"Diesel, I'm not here about your club. You have to believe me."

His eyes locked on mine as he replied, "I want to believe you, and in my gut, I think you're telling the truth."

"Good." The conversation had grown heavy, and it was starting to wear on me. Hoping to change the subject, I said, "Since your memory is still intact, why don't you tell me something about yourself."

"What do you want to know?"

"Anything. Everything. Where do you live? What do you do for a living? Are you married? Things like that."

"I live here in Port Angeles, and I ..."

"Wait. We're in Port Angeles, Washington?"

"Yeah. Do you remember being here?"

While the name seemed familiar, I couldn't actually remember ever being here before. I tried to think where I might've heard it, but nothing came to me. "I don't think so."

"Well, you're here now."

"Good to know," I mumbled. "Just keep going. I'm sorry I interrupted."

"Okay. Let's see." His eyes skirted up to the ceiling as

he thought about how to continue, then he said, "I work with the brothers down at the construction company, and I help out at the garage when I can. And I'm not married … not even close."

A peculiar sense of relief trickled over me when he mentioned that he wasn't married. I tried to convince myself that the feeling was just a side effect of the medication Doc had given me and not the fact that he was so good-looking. A twinge of guilt tugged at me when I realized I had no idea if there was anyone special in my life. I lifted my left hand, checking for a ring, and even though there wasn't one, I felt an odd sensation when I ran my thumb across the bottom of my index finger. For all I knew, I was happily married, and on top of that, I could've had children. The last thing I needed to do was sit there ogling some sexy biker while my family could be home waiting for me. The thought saddened me. How could I have forgotten something so important. I laid my head back on the pillow and sighed.

"Why don't you get some rest? It might do you some good."

I wasn't sure I could sleep, especially knowing that Cotton and the others were just outside that door, so I looked at him and asked, "You're staying here, right?"

"Yes, angel. I'm not going anywhere. Now, get some sleep."

I closed my eyes, and with Diesel sitting beside me, I was able to relax enough to drift off. I don't know how long I'd been sleeping, when I heard a *something* calling out to me from the darkness. I couldn't make out his face, but I could hear a man pleading, "I'm sorry, sweetheart.

I'm so, so sorry. You know I didn't mean it. I'll never hurt you again. I promise. You have to forgive me."

There was something familiar about his voice, something that made me feel anxious, and I wanted to get away from him. That feeling only got worse when his tone suddenly changed. My heart started to race as he growled, "Where you going to go? Huh? That's right. You've got no place to go now, do ya? I'm all you got, so just stop all this bullshit and come home. It's not like you have a fucking choice."

DIESEL

I'd been sitting there for over an hour just watching her sleep, and I couldn't take my eyes off of her. Even though I knew nothing about this woman, I was utterly captivated by her. I wanted to know everything about her, which was frustrating as hell since she couldn't tell me a damn thing—not even her goddamn name. It was in my nature to want to fix things, and I felt completely helpless as I sat there staring at her. Just as I leaned back in my chair, I heard her whimper, and then her head started to rock from side to side. At first, she just mumbled incoherently under her breath, but then the rhythm of her breathing changed to a rapid pace. Her entire body grew stiff as she let out a remorseful moan. Realizing she was having a bad dream, I got up and placed my hand on her arm.

"It's okay. It's just a dream." Her eyes shot open and tears started to stream down her face. "Are you okay?"

"I don't know," she cried. "It was just a dream, but it felt so real."

"What was the dream about?"

"I … can't remember exactly … There was a man talking to me. At first, he was apologizing for something he'd done. He kept saying he was sorry, but then … I don't know. He seemed so angry … hateful. He told me I had to come home."

"Do you think you knew the man in the dream?"

Her voice wavered as she said, "Maybe, but I can't say for sure. It might've been nothing more than just a dream."

"But it could've been something else," I pushed. "Are you sure you can't remember anything more? Did the man say your name or anything that might help trigger your memory?"

"No, just that I had to come home because I had nowhere else to go."

"Any idea where home might be?"

I could hear the frustration in her voice when she answered, "I already told you *no*."

I hated that I'd upset her, and I was just about to apologize when Doc walked in. As he started towards us, he asked her, "How are you feeling?"

"A little better, I guess."

"And the pain? You still doing okay with that or should I give you another round of pain relievers?"

"I think I'm good for now," she answered. "It doesn't hurt as bad when I breathe, so things are looking up."

"Good to hear." Doc glanced over to me. "I talked to Cotton, and he's got a room set up for her. Wanna help me get her moved?"

"Yeah. I can do that."

"Should I get a wheelchair, or are you good to walk?"

"I think I can walk," she replied and sat up on the bed. I moved beside her, slipping my arm around her waist, and helped her to her feet. As soon as I did, I noticed her wince. "You okay?"

She gave me a quick nod, and we started towards the door. I held her close to my side, following Doc down the hallway until he stopped in front of the empty room across the hall from mine and opened the door. "Here we go."

I helped her inside and over to the bed. Once she was sitting down, I pulled the covers back and eased them over her legs. "Thank you, Diesel."

"No problem."

"I've been thinking ... We need something to call you until you remember your name. Got any ideas?"

"Do you think you can come up with something better than the name ... *Diesel*?" She teased.

"Hey, I take offense to that." I chuckled.

"You know I'm just messing with you. Besides, I don't know the first thing about nicknames and all that. So, whatever you think will be fine."

Trying my best to get back at her, I suggested, "How about Dori? You know, that fish from that kids' movie who's always forgetting everything?"

She laughed, then added, "How about Demi, for dementia?"

"Or Abby, for absentminded?"

"How about Daisy, for dazed and confused?" I suggested with a chuckle.

Laughter filled the room and my chest tightened when I noticed how beautiful she looked when she smiled. I was staring at her with wonder and almost missed it when she said, "There's always Amy, for amnesia."

Doc waved his hand in the air, stopping our little exchange as he said, "Let's not get carried away, you two. We need to keep it simple. Something that won't cause disassociation later. How about for now we call you, *Lucky*? Considering all you've been through, I'd say the name fits."

"Lucky." She paused for a moment as she considered the name. "I like it."

"I do, too." The irony of that name was not lost on me as I thought of my father's fate.

Doc patted me on the shoulder. "I'm glad you agree. Now, why don't you go take a break? Go grab a bite to eat or something while I check her bandages."

"Okay." As I started for the door, I turned to her and asked, "Can I get you anything?"

"Maybe something to drink?"

Doc shook his head. "Get her some of that soup Cass made for her, and maybe a sandwich. We need to get some real food in her system."

"You got it," I told him and walked out the door.

The smell of freshly cooked biscuits lingered down the hall as I went into the kitchen, and when I walked inside, I found Cass standing at the stove. She was Cotton's ol' lady and the queen of the house, so it came as no surprise that she was getting lunch ready for the crew. I strolled over to where Cass was stirring something simmering in a pot, and as I peered over her shoulder, I asked, "What's for lunch?"

Smiling, she answered, "I made pork chops, mashed

potatoes, and biscuits for you boys, and I've warmed up some soup for our guest if she's up for it."

"I think she's up for it. It would do her good to eat something."

Just as Cass was about to respond, Zoe walked in with Two Bit, and as soon as I saw the smile on her face, I was hit with a sense of pride knowing that my sister was truly happy. I hadn't seen either of them since I'd left for Memphis, so I wasn't surprised when Two Bit asked, "How was the trip?"

"Long, but we got the job done."

"Knew you would. Heard you've been keeping an eye out on our little guest."

"I have."

"Have you been able to find out anything about her?" Zoe asked as she went over to help Cass fix our plates.

I looked at Zoe and answered, "No, not yet."

"I can't imagine being out there in all that snow like that. She must've been frozen to the core." She started piling food on her man's plate and then glanced back at me. "Must be a real fighter to survive all that."

"Damn straight. I don't know too many men who could've made it through that kind of blizzard," Two Bit added.

"I reckon so."

As Cass handed me my plate, she said, "If there's anything I can do to help with her, just let me know."

"You know I will."

Starving, I sat down at the table and dug in; after several bites, I actually moaned, "Damn, Cass. This is incredible."

"Thanks, hon." She laughed. "Glad you like it." Once I was done, she handed me a bowl of soup to take to Lucky.

As the next few days rolled by, it was more of the same. Since Cotton wanted someone looking after Lucky at all times, one of the prospects would keep watch by her door at night, while I stayed with her during the day. I kept hoping that a new memory might unfold during our time together, but nothing ever came. Since she seemed to be getting a little stronger, I was expecting to see more progress, and I wasn't the only one. All the brothers, especially Cotton, wanted to know what had happened to her and how she'd ended up on our doorstep, but like me, they would just have to wait. I honestly didn't mind; I'd take any excuse to spend time with her.

We'd just decided to start a movie when Doc came in to check her bandages. I sat over in the corner and watched as he slowly unwound the large, white gauze from around her head; once it was removed, he smiled and said, "Well, look at that. I'd say it's healing up real nice there, darlin'."

"That's good news."

"It is. I think we're gonna go without the bandage for now. You good with that?" he asked.

"Yes. I'm definitely good with that," she told him with excitement. "Does that mean I can actually take a shower and wash my hair?"

"I think that would be okay. I'm sure we could get Cass to help and maybe get you some fresh clothes."

"That would be wonderful. Like *unbelievably wonderful*." She smiled. "I can't thank you enough for everything you all have done for me."

Hearing how excited she was, I headed out to find Cass. As expected, she was tickled to give her a hand, and after she gathered up some fresh clothes, she went to help Lucky get showered and dressed. After an hour of who knows what, the bathroom door opened, and the room was suddenly filled with a warm scent of vanilla and lavender. My eyes were glued to the doorway, and when Lucky finally stepped into view, the sight of her took my breath away. She was just wearing a t-shirt and sweats, but she was absolutely the most beautiful thing I'd ever seen. Her dark brown hair was long with subtle waves that flowed down past her delicate shoulders, and her eyes sparkled with intrigue as she watched my reaction to her newly refreshed look. Noting my enamored expression, Cass smiled knowingly. "Lucky is quite the beauty, wouldn't you say?"

"Um-hmm." It took me a moment to pull myself together, but once I did, I asked her, "How are you feeling after your shower?"

"Much better. Thanks." She looked over to Cass and said, "I really appreciate you helping me do all this."

"No problem, sweetie. If you need anything else, just give me a shout. I've got to get going. Cotton is waiting for me back at the house." As she started for the door, Cass turned to me and said, "You two try and behave yourselves tonight."

Knowing she was just giving me a hard time, I rolled my eyes and replied, "I don't think that'll be a problem, Cass."

Once she was gone, Lucky walked with caution over to the bed and sat down. "Are you still up for watching a movie or something?"

"Sure. We can do that." I grabbed the chair and

brought it closer to the bed, sitting it down next to her. "Why don't you see what's on?"

She reached for the remote and started flipping through the channels until she finally landed on some action movie. "Is this okay?"

"It's perfect."

Nestling herself under the covers, it wasn't long before she'd drifted off to sleep. Not wanting to disturb her, I turned the volume down, leaned back in my chair, and continued to watch the movie. Once it ended, another began, and just as it was starting to get interesting, I noticed that Lucky was having one of her dreams again. At first her whimpers were soft and muted, but they quickly escalated into something more. Her head thrashed from side to side as she cried, "No. Please. Stop!"

I got up and sat on the edge of the bed as I placed my hands on her shoulders, gently shaking her. "Lucky. Wake up. You're dreaming."

Her arms started flailing about, and then her hands clenched into fists as she started wailing into me. "Let me go! Get away from me!"

"Lucky!" Grabbing her wrists, I tried to restrain her as I spoke firmly, "Wake up! It's me, Diesel."

Her eyes flew open, and a panicked look crossed her face as she stared up at me. She inhaled a quick breath as she cried, "What happened?"

"You were having another bad dream," I told her as I released her wrists. "But it's over now. You're okay."

The fear in her eyes started to fade as she looked up at me, and without warning, she sat up and wrapped her arms around me, hugging me tightly. "It felt so real."

As I held her close, I asked, "Do you remember anything that happened?"

"There was a man. He was hitting me … over and over again … and he was saying all these awful things to me."

Over the past few days, she'd had several nightmares similar to this one, so I had to ask, "Was it the same man as before?"

Her voice trembled as she answered, "Yes. I think so."

I wanted to push her to see if she could remember something more, but when I saw the tears streaming down her face, I couldn't force myself do it. She was just too distraught, and I was overcome with the need to take her pain away. I brought my hands up to her face as I said, "I don't know who this man is or what he did to you, but he's not going to hurt you again. I give you my word on that."

"Why would he want to hurt me? What could I have done to him to make him so angry?"

"There's nothing in this world that you could do to deserve someone putting their hands on you, angel. You know that, right?"

She shrugged. "I guess."

"There's no guessing about it. No one *ever* has the right to hurt you." We sat there silently for several minutes, and it was clear from the look in her eyes that she was exhausted. Hoping that she might be able to rest, I said, "Why don't you lay back down and try to go back to sleep."

She nodded, and once she was settled back in the bed, I sent a message to Doc telling him to come to the room. Once he'd arrived, I informed him about the dreams she'd been having and asked him to sit with her while I went to talk to Cotton. Without question, he agreed, and I left in search of Cotton. It was late, so I was surprised to find that he was still in his office, sitting at his desk. As soon as I knocked on his door, he looked at me and asked, "You got some news with the girl?"

"Yes and no," I told him as I stepped inside his office. "She still can't remember her name or where she came from, but she's having these fucked up dreams."

"What kind of dreams?"

"The kind where some guy is beating the hell out of her." I went on, "It would explain all the old scars. Maybe it was an old boyfriend or—"

"It could've been anyone. That's the problem, Diesel. For all we know, it could've been someone close to her, or it could've been another club using her as a plant."

"Do you really think it's possible that she's with another club?"

He shrugged. "It's unlikely, but we've got to play this thing safe, brother. We can't take any chances until we know what's going on with her."

"I understand, but I gotta tell ya … there's someone in those dreams who's scaring the hell out of her."

"This weather should be clearing out in the next day or two; hopefully, once the roads are in better shape, we can get out there and find *something* that'll give us some answers." He leaned back in his chair as he looked at me and said, "For now, keep doing what you're doing. Maybe one of those damn nightmares will help her remember something."

"You got it."

As I started for the door, Cotton called out to me. "Diesel?"

"Yeah?"

"Be careful with this girl. For all we know she's got a whole other life out there … a family, kids … a *husband*. You don't want to find yourself in a situation that's hard to get out of, if you know what I mean."

I nodded, and without saying a word, I left. There was nothing I could say anyway. I knew exactly what he meant, but it was too late. I was already in too deep.

ELLIE

It had been days since my accident, and Doc no longer believed that my amnesia had anything to do with my concussion. After Diesel told him about the nightmares I've been having, he decided that my lack of memory was my mind's way of protecting me from whatever had happened to me. At first, I thought he was wrong, but when I saw the scars that marked my body, I started to think differently. I couldn't imagine how I'd acquired so many injuries, unless my dreams weren't actually dreams. I spent hours trying to force myself to remember something, *anything*. I needed to find the answers that were hidden away in the back of my mind, but all I found were more questions. It was utterly exhausting, and when I couldn't take it a moment longer, I curled up into a ball and tried to get some sleep. Like many times before, just as I started to drift off, I felt myself being pulled into a place where I didn't want to be. I was standing in darkness with the sound of his voice echoing through the room.

"*Every goddamn day*, it's always the same thing with you. You're always running your fucking mouth about something," he barked.

"I … uh …" I stammered.

"What? Spit it out, you stupid piece of shit, or better yet, don't!" He reared his hand back and slammed it across my cheek, busting open my bottom lip.

I felt the blood trickle from my mouth as I brought my hand up to my face. I tried to force myself to look at him, but I was too scared. When he started shouting again, I realized that not knowing what was causing me such heartache and pain was much more terrifying than seeing it right in front of my face, so I raised my head to look at him. That's when I saw his angry, black eyes staring back at me. "What? You got something to say, bitch?"

"Who are you?" I mumbled.

"Who am I?" He laughed maniacally, then charged towards me as he growled, "I'm your worst fucking nightmare!"

He wrapped his hands around my neck, and as he stood there choking me, his lips curled into a wicked smile. He tightened his hold, then brought his mouth to my ear and whispered, "You're pathetic. Why don't you do us both a favor and just fucking die?"

My heart raced as I tugged at his hands, and just as I felt myself start to fade away, I inhaled a deep breath and sat up in the bed. I was still gasping when Diesel came charging into the room. "Are you okay?"

I held my hand up, letting him know I needed a minute, and once I was able to collect myself, I threw the covers back and stood up. "I need to get out of here. *Please*."

"Okay. We can do that," he answered calmly. "You want to grab something to eat?"

"I'm not really hungry."

I could see the concern in his eyes as he led me out of the room, and I wasn't sure if he knew where he should take me as we started down the hall. I'd only been out a couple of times, when I'd gone to the kitchen for a bite to eat or down to the infirmary with Doc, so I really hadn't gotten a chance to see much of the clubhouse. Since I'd been there, it had been relatively quiet, making me wonder what these men did during the day. I could only assume that they had their own lives outside of the club, working and spending time with their families. My curiosity got the best of me, and I found myself trying to peek into the different rooms as we walked by. Unfortunately, most of the doors were closed, so I couldn't see much. As we started down a second hall, I could hear voices rumbling, and it only got louder as we continued walking. When we finally stopped, Diesel opened a large door, and the sounds of children's laughter came barreling out. I stepped inside and found several kids sitting on a big, L-shaped sofa, and they were playing some video game on the large TV that was mounted on the wall.

We stood and watched them for a moment, and I couldn't help but smile as I watched the young, blond-headed boy with Down Syndrome twist and turn in his seat as he tried to keep his guy on the screen in motion while the boy on the end shouted different directions to the girl sitting between them. She was a good amount older than them, maybe thirteen or fourteen, and she was beautiful. Her eyebrows furrowed as her character fell off the mountain and faded away. When they started arguing back and forth, Diesel walked over to them and said, "Hey, Dusty. Who's winning?"

His eyes lit up with pride as he announced, "I'm beating Lauren."

The little boy at the other end of the sofa looked over to Diesel and said, "She won the last game, though."

"What about you, Wyatt? Have you been playing?"

"No," Lauren answered for him. "He's been too busy telling me how to play."

"I'd like you all to meet a friend of mine." When he motioned his hand in my direction, they all turned to look at me with little frowns on their faces. "This is Lucky."

"Is she the one who's been sick?" Wyatt asked.

"Yeah, but she's feeling better now." He smiled as he continued, "We're going to play a game of pool. Do any of you want to play with us?"

In unison, they all answered, "No, thank you."

"Okay, then. Your loss."

He walked over to the pool table, and as he started lining up the balls, I told him, "I don't know how to play pool."

"That's okay." He gave me a wink. "I'll teach you."

He walked over and took two pool sticks down from the rack and handed one to me. "Now, what?"

"Now, you watch as I break." There was something about the way he smiled that made me instantly feel at ease, and I found myself drawn to him in a way I hadn't expected. I'd thought he was attractive from the start. Who wouldn't? The guy was every girl's dream with his tall, muscular build and chiseled jaw, but his wicked good looks weren't the only thing that drew me to him. It was the way he made me feel. With just a touch of his hand, the low, sexy sound of his voice, or an unexpected smile, he could make me forget the hell I was going through. I watched as he leaned over the table and rested the end of the stick on the curve of his thumb, sliding it quickly towards the white ball. It rushed forward and slammed into the other balls, causing them to disperse across the table. When one of the striped balls fell into the pocket, he looked over to me and announced, "I'm stripes."

After he moved to the other end of the table and prepared to take another shot, I said, "I think you have an unfair advantage."

Smiling, he made his play and when he missed his mark, I knew he'd done it on purpose. "Your turn."

"I think I'll just watch you."

"Come on." He motioned me over to him. "You can do this."

"If you say so." I stepped over to the table with the pool stick in my hand and tried to position myself where I might actually be able to hit the white ball with the small end of the stick. As I leaned towards the table, my focus was on the ball, and I didn't realize that Diesel had come up behind me. When he reached around me to help, he caught me by surprise, and I yelped. With my heart racing, I jumped back like I'd been hit by lightning, and as I clung to the pool stick, I tried to calm the panic that was rushing through my veins. I had no idea why I'd reacted like that, and as soon as the fear started to subside, it was replaced with embarrassment.

"Hey, I'm sorry about that. I was just trying to help. Are you okay?"

"Um … yeah. I don't know what that was all about."

Diesel had been nothing but a gentleman to me since the moment we'd met, and I hated that I made him think he'd done something wrong. "I guess I wasn't expecting you to come up behind me. I'm sorry."

"Nothing for you to be sorry about, angel. I should've given you a heads up."

I put the pool stick down. "Maybe this wasn't a good idea."

"Sure, it was. You'll see," he assured me. "Now, grab that stick and give it another try." He held up his hands and smiled as he teased. "I'll stay over here and keep my hands to myself."

And just like that, he'd managed to get me back on track. I walked back over to the table, and as I took the pool stick back in my hand, I tried my best to make the shot. To my surprise, the ball dropped into the pocket. My mouth fell open, and I turned to him with disbelief. "Did you see that?"

"I did. Now, do it again."

Each time I prepared to take my shot, he'd do his best to give me pointers, but he did it at a distance. When it was his turn, I found myself watching his every move—the way he cocked his eyebrow as he studied the ball, the sway of his hip when he made his shot, and the sexy smirk that crossed his face when the ball slipped into the side pocket. Diesel got to me in ways I couldn't begin to explain. Being with him made me forget that I was the girl who had no name—along with a past I couldn't remember. As I stood there staring at him, I realized that there was a positive side to not being able to remember who I was. I was given the chance to be whatever I wanted to be, and at that moment, I just wanted to be happy.

Just as we were finishing our game, Lauren came over to the table and asked, "Can I play?"

"You tired of playing Mario?" Diesel asked.

"No. I'm tired of listening to them argue." She let out a huff and added, "They're as bad as listening to Cotton and Maverick fight about football."

"Damn. That's pretty bad." Diesel chuckled as he handed her the pool stick. "Why don't you take the next shot and show Lucky here how it's done."

With a look of determination, she leaned over the table and took her shot, landing the ball straight into the side pocket. Lauren repeated the same move for the next three shots, ending the game with a huge win. "How's that?"

"That was amazing!" I answered.

"Cotton taught me how to play. He's the best."

"That he is," Diesel agreed. "You want another go?"

"Sure."

We started another game, and it wasn't long before the boys came over to join us. After several plays, the boys took over our game, leaving Diesel and I sitting to the side watching as they both tried to beat Lauren. Unfortunately for them, she couldn't be beat. When they started a second game, Diesel leaned over to me and asked, "How 'bout we go grab something to eat?"

"Sounds good to me."

"Thank God. Not sure how much more of this I can take." He took my hand in his and led me towards the door. Before we walked out, he turned to them and said, "Try not to kill each other while we're gone."

"We won't," Wyatt promised.

When we got to the kitchen, Diesel made his way over

to the refrigerator and asked, "What are you in the mood for?"

"Anything is fine."

He looked over his shoulder as he asked, "Are you always so easy to please?"

"I don't know. I can't remember." I teased him.

"Oh, yeah. Well, something tells me that kind of thing sticks with a person whether they can remember their name or not."

"You think so?"

"Absolutely." He pulled out a pan of lasagna, and as he cut each of us a piece, he said, "I figure it's like that with lots of stuff."

"Such as?"

"You know. The fundamentals of someone's personality. Their likes and dislikes. The side of the bed you sleep on. Stuff like that." He put the plate in the microwave, then he continued, "It's not like you're suddenly going to start loving broccoli when you spent your whole life hating it."

"I guess that makes sense." I went to the cabinet and got each of us a glass, then filled them with ice water. After I put them on the table, I asked, "Do you like broccoli?"

"Not a fan. Don't like asparagus either."

"What side of the bed do you sleep on?"

He thought for a moment, then he said, "The side closest to the door."

"So, it's all about the door and not really the side?" I asked.

"I hadn't really thought about it, but yeah. I like being

close to an exit in case something happens. Quick escape and all."

Once the lasagna was warmed up, he brought it over to the table, and we both sat down. We'd just started to eat, when I looked over to him and asked, "Can I ask you a question?"

"Sure. Whatcha got on your mind?"

"What makes someone decide to be part of a motorcycle club?"

"It's different for everyone, but for me, I like the comradery that comes with being part of the brotherhood. It's hard to explain, really. I had a good family life and all that, but I never really felt like I fit anywhere. I fit here. And at the end of the day, I know they have my back, and they know I have theirs. It's not always sunshine and daisies, especially this crew, but there's no other place I'd rather be."

"What about your *real family*? Where are they now?"

"Both of my parents are gone. I still talk to my stepdad from time to time, but after mom got cancer and passed away, we aren't as close as we used to be. He got remarried and seems to be happy with his new life."

"I'm really sorry to hear about your mom."

"That was a long time ago."

"What about your real dad? What happened with him?"

"Well, that's kind of a long story."

"I'd like to hear it if you don't mind sharing."

DIESEL

I told Lucky everything, including my time with the Chosen. I'm not sure what compelled me to divulge so much about myself, but once I started, I didn't stop until I'd gotten it all out. She was just so easy to talk to, and I never once saw a flicker of judgement when I spoke. I'd never met anyone quite like her. After all she's been through, I would expect her to be guarded, to surround herself in a protective wall and not let anyone get close to her, but when she was with me, there were no walls. It was just her and I, and with every new moment we were together, we grew closer. It all seemed so strange to me. She didn't even have a name, but she was more real to me than any woman I'd ever met. I wanted to keep her close and protect her because the mere thought of someone hurting her drove me insane. As we sat there talking, I vowed to myself that I would do everything in my power to keep her safe.

After we finished eating, I took her back to her room,

and I was about to head back to my own so she could get settled when she got a funny look on her face. "What's wrong?"

"I hate to ask since you've been stuck with me all day, but can you stay with me for just a little while longer ... just until I fall asleep?"

"You worried you're gonna have another bad dream?"

"A little bit. That last one really got to me. I was hoping if you'd stay, I might not *have* another one. I know one of the guys usually sits outside in the hall and watches over things, but it's just not the same as having you in here with me," she confessed.

I knew those nightmares had been wearing on her, and I couldn't blame her for being worried. Hell, I was worried myself. After seeing how upset they'd made her, I'd made a habit of checking in on her every night to make sure she was okay. I hoped that she was right and my staying might stop them from coming, even if it was just for a little while, so I answered, "Of course."

I walked over and sat down in the chair at the foot of her bed, and once I was settled, she turned to face the wall. I listened as her breathing became shallow, and I thought she had gone to sleep, until she asked, "Would you mind lying down next to me?"

"What?"

"Will you lie down with me?" she asked again.

"You sure about that?"

Without turning to look at me, she replied, "I'm just so tired of feeling lost and alone ... I don't want to feel alone right now."

I knew it wasn't a good idea. I'd already started to have

feelings for her, feelings I had no business having, and being in that bed with her was just going to make them harder to ignore. But after hearing the vulnerability in her voice, there was no way I could turn her down. I got up from the chair and walked over to the bed, carefully settling in next to her. I leaned my head back on the pillow and tried to pretend that she wasn't there, but my body knew. Just like every time before, as soon as I got close to her, I felt a rush that made it damn near impossible not to reach for her, take her in my arms, and show her how much I wanted her. But I knew that wasn't an option, not now—not when there was so much uncertainty surrounding her. Trying my best not to disturb her, I turned to look at her, and she hadn't moved. She stayed planted in her spot until she finally drifted off to sleep. I laid there for several hours, simply listening to the rhythm of her breathing, and without realizing what I was doing, I fell sound asleep.

I woke up the next morning with Lucky's beautiful, dark eyes staring at me. She was propped up on her elbow, and she smiled. "Good morning."

"Good morning." I sat up and rubbed the sleep out of my eyes. "I must've fallen asleep. I didn't mean to stay the night in your bed."

"That's okay." A light blush crossed her face as she added, "It was nice having you here."

"Were you able to get any sleep?"

"Yeah. I slept great. Better than I have in days"

"Well, that's good to hear." I smiled as I told her, "I was afraid my snoring might've kept you awake."

"I'm pretty sure I was the one who was snoring, but thanks for not noticing."

"Never said I didn't notice. You snore with the best of them. Pretty sure you've got the rest of the guys beat in that department." I teased.

"Seriously?"

"Yep." I got out of the bed and stretched. "I need a hot shower and some coffee. How about you?"

"Sounds good to me."

"Good." As I headed for the door, I told her, "I'll be back as soon as I get out of the shower."

"Okay."

I'd just gotten dressed and was on my way to get Lucky when I spotted Two Bit heading towards me. He was known for saying whatever was on his mind, and from the expression on his face, it was clear that he had something to say. With his eyebrow cocked, he announced, "We found something."

"What?" He motioned for me to go with him, and as I followed him down the hall, I anxiously asked, "What the hell did you find?"

"A car," he answered as he walked into the bar.

Maverick and Stitch were at one of the back tables talking with Cotton, and as soon as we walked up, I heard Maverick say, "We tried, but with all the snow and ice, we just couldn't get down there."

"Hell, the damn thing is almost a hundred feet down the ravine. Even if there wasn't any snow, I don't know how we'd get to it without some help."

"Do you think the car is Lucky's?"

Maverick turned to me and answered, "Yeah, but we won't know for sure until we can get down there and check it out."

"Where is it?"

Stitch cleared his throat as he crossed his arms. As the club's enforcer, he was always thinking one step ahead, and his voice was deep and methodical as he answered, "About three miles east of here—at Eagle's point. She must've lost control around that curve and flipped over the embankment. The car is pretty fucked up. It's a fuckin' miracle she made it out of there alive."

Every ounce of empathy I had kicked in as I asked, "She walked for three miles in that storm?"

"Apparently so." Cotton's eyes were filled with concern. "Looks like she was running from something after all."

"The question is, from what? Or better yet, *from who?*" Maverick asked.

"Hopefully, we'll find some answers in that car." Cotton turned to Maverick and said, "Get with Guardrail and see what equipment he has that might help us get down there."

Guardrail was the club's VP, and he was also the front man for the club's construction company. If anyone had something that would help us, it would be him, so I wasn't surprised when Maverick replied, "Already did. He said he could have us something here by noon."

Cotton shook his head. "Gonna need to be sooner than that. We need to get to it before someone else does."

"I'll call him back." He stepped to the side and dialed his number. After talking to him for just a few minutes, he hung up the phone and turned back to us. "He'll be here in two hours.

"Good. Meet back here at ten, and then we'll head over there. And dress warm. It's cold as shit out there," Cotton ordered.

After we dispersed, I went down the hall towards Lucky's room where I found Drake, one of our prospects, standing by her door. "Morning, Diesel. How's it going, brother?"

"It's going. You?"

"Better now that it stopped fucking snowing. Hell, I thought that storm would never pass."

"I hear ya." I nodded towards the door. "Is Lucky in there?"

"Yep."

I knocked on her door, and as I waited for her to answer, I considered telling her about the car. I thought it might lift her spirits but decided against it, thinking I didn't want her to be disappointed if it turned out to be nothing. When she opened the door, I asked, "You ready to grab a bite to eat?"

"Not at the moment." She motioned to a small tray of food behind her. "Cass already brought me something."

"Oh. Okay." I turned back and made sure that Drake was still close by. "I've got some things to take care of for a few hours, but Cass or Doc will be around if you need anything."

"I'll be fine. Cass brought me some magazines to read, so I'll just hang out here until you get back."

"I'll be back soon," I told her as I made my way down the hallway towards the kitchen. I didn't like that she couldn't contact me if she needed me, so I'd need to talk to Cotton about getting her a burner phone. But that would have to wait until later. For now, I needed to get some food in my stomach and then meet the guys to go check out that car. When I walked into the kitchen, Stitch and Maverick were already sitting down at the table, eating their eggs and drinking their coffee, while Two Bit and Clutch were at the stove, filling their plates with food. I walked over and poured myself a cup of coffee before going over to the stove to get my food. Once I'd made my plate, I went over and joined the others at the table.

Without talking to anyone in particular, Maverick said, "Henley and Cass tried to take Thomas sledding yesterday, but Henley said he wasn't having any part of it. She sat him on her lap, and when they went down that little hill in front of the house, he pitched an ever lovin' fit."

He'd married Henley before I was even associated with the club, but I didn't have to be around from the beginning to know that they were crazy about each other—and they absolutely adored their two-year-old son, Thomas. Clutch laughed as he said, "Sounds like he takes after his old man."

"The hell you say. I used to love to go sledding when I was a kid. There wasn't a hill I wouldn't try," he argued.

"Give him time," Stitch told him. "He'll be out there scaring the shit out of you before you know it."

"What about Mia? Does she like the snow?" Clutch asked.

"Nope. She's not a fan either, but Wyatt seems to like it … at least for a little while."

I sat there listening to them talk about their kids, and as always, I was amazed to see the softer side of the very men who I knew could be hard as nails. Hell, Stitch could bring the strongest men to their knees without breaking a sweat, but when he talked about his kids, he looked like an average Joe. We'd been sitting there talking for almost an hour when I heard Cass say, "Guys. You need to come see this."

We all turned, and when found her standing in the doorway with a panicked look on her face, we all got up and followed her into the TV room. I had no idea what was going on until I heard Cass say, "Isn't that Lucky?"

I looked up at the television, and as soon as I saw those beautiful, dark eyes staring back at me, I knew it was her. My breath caught in my throat as I read the word *MISSING* written in bold red letters above her picture, and when I started searching for her name, my heart dropped to the pit of my stomach when I noticed the picture of the man next to her. Without reading any further, I knew it was her husband. Fuck.

"Yep, that's her," Maverick announced.

I ignored him as I listened to the news anchor describe how Brady and Ellie Blackwell had been declared missing after neither one of them had shown up for work. She stated that the police had begun an investigation, but as of yet, they had found no leads. My mind was reeling as I listened to her say that Brady Blackwell's father, Police Chief Grayson Blackwell, had offered a reward for any information regarding the couple's whereabouts. When she finally finished talking, I turned to my brothers and said, "This doesn't make any fucking sense. If they're both missing, how the hell did she end up here?"

"She's the only one who can answer that, brother," Stitch replied. "And if the cops are looking for her, it's only a matter of time before they start sniffing around here."

"You got that right," Cotton grumbled as he shook his

head. "Especially if that's her car in the ravine. Either way, we need to be prepared. Consider us on high alert."

Maverick stepped forward and said, "Is there a reason why we're putting our necks out for this chick? Hell, we don't know anything about her."

Without batting an eye, Cotton replied, "Fate brought her to our doorstep, and we chose to take her in. We're not turning our backs on her now. We're going to see this thing though."

His words proved once again that Cotton was a man of honor, making me proud to be his brother. I glanced back up at the screen, and as I stared at her picture, I muttered, "Ellie Blackwell."

Hearing me, Clutch replied, "And Brady Blackwell. The chick's married, Diesel."

"I'm not buying it, Clutch. Something about this just doesn't feel right."

"I guess there's only one way for you to find out."

With that, I turned and went straight to her room. When I got to her door, I took a deep breath, and after I knocked, she answered, "It's open."

I opened the door and found her sitting Indian style at the foot of her bed. Her hair was pulled up on top of her head in a messy bun, and she was wearing one of my t-shirts that was at least two sizes too big for her. There was a magazine in her lap, and when she looked up and saw me standing there, a smile spread across her face. Breathtaking. She was absolutely breathtaking.

She cocked her head to the side and said, "That was fast. I wasn't expecting you until later."

I didn't respond. I couldn't. What I wanted more than anything else was sitting right there in front of me, and the thought that she might belong to another made my blood run cold. I didn't want to lose her, not like this. But then, I couldn't lose what I never had, and I couldn't keep what wasn't mine. Noticing my struggle, her smile quickly faded. "Is everything okay?"

I'd wanted to ease my way into it, but the words just rolled right off my tongue. "Are you Ellie Blackwell?"

ELLIE

I never would've dreamed that two little words could have such an earth-shattering effect on me. As soon as he said the name *Ellie Blackwell*, everything around me stood still. It sounded so familiar, like it was something that belonged to me, but it was just out of reach. I couldn't think of anything beyond *yes, that is my name*, but I knew there was more. My mind started racing, and with each breath I took, a new memory would come rushing back—the very memories that my mind had tried to protect me from, and a feeling of desperation washed over me. I could only remember tiny bits and pieces that would quickly float off in the distance, and I wanted to grab a hold of each and every one of them. I needed to make sense of the confusion that had come with the sound of my name. I needed to know how I ended up at the Satan's Fury clubhouse, but those memories were still stubbornly tucked away in the back of my mind, refusing to be found. I lowered my head into my hands and sobbed helplessly as Diesel came over and sat down next to me. I knew he was waiting for my response, but I was too distraught to form the words.

He placed the palm of his hand on my back and slowly ran it up and down my spine. "I know you're scared, but you've gotta face this thing head on. You've gotta understand the fear for what it is and find a way to get through it. You've done it before, but this time, you don't have to do it alone. I'm right here with you, and I'm not going anywhere."

I could tell by the sound of his voice that he meant what he said, and I felt a sense of strength knowing that he'd be there by my side. I inhaled a deep breath as I wiped the tears from my eyes and turned to look at him. "I'm Ellie Blackwell."

"They just showed a picture of you on the news. The reporter said that you're missing, and so is *your husband ... Brady.* The cops are looking for both of you."

Brady. My stomach twisted into knots at the sound of his name. For days, I'd been dreaming about him, about the abuse, the torture, and the pain. I'd prayed that it was all just some crazy nightmare, but it wasn't just a nightmare—it was my life. While there were things I could remember about our apartment, my job at the coffee shop, and the never-ending battles with Brady, there was still so much that I couldn't piece together. "I don't know where he is."

"There are people out there looking for you, including the police. I'd say we should let them know where you are and see if we can find something out about him, but I keep thinking about something Maverick said."

"What?"

"When they found you out there in the snow, you were

barely hanging on. Maverick told me that Cotton wanted to take you to the hospital, but you begged him not to. He said you were adamant about it, but passed out before you could tell them why. Do you have any idea what that was about?"

I tried to think back on that night, but I drew a blank. It was like a chunk of time was simply gone, and I had no idea how to get it back. "No. That part hasn't come back to me yet."

"What can you remember?"

"Just fragments of my life ... Some seem clearer than others." I sighed. "I remember marrying Brady right out of high school. I was pregnant and thought I was doing the right thing. It turns out I was wrong."

While he tried to hide it, I could hear the disappointment in his voice when he asked, "So, you've got a kid?"

I felt the tears threatening to fall all over again as I murmured, "No."

His eyebrows furrowed with confusion. "But ... you said you were pregnant."

"I was, but I lost her after one of Brady's bad days." My eyes dropped to my lap. "It was the first time, but it wasn't the last."

"So, the dreams?"

Feeling embarrassed and ashamed, I answered, "Yeah. That was Brady."

The room fell silent as both of us sat there lost in our own world of thoughts. I took a deep, cleansing breath and tried to focus on remembering the parts that hadn't returned, and less on the ones that had. It wasn't just *that night* that I couldn't remember. There were more empty spaces, more lapses in time that I had absolutely no recollection, and that worried me. The fact that there was still so much I couldn't remember made me worry that the worst was yet to come. Filled with panic, I glanced over at Diesel, and he looked like he was in another world. I had no idea what he was thinking, but it was clear from his expression that he was upset.

After several long moments, he finally growled, "He did that to you, and he was a fucking cop. He should've done everything in his power to protect you and keep you safe, but …"

"There's no use in trying to make sense of it, Diesel. The whole thing was completely unbelievable. I never dreamed that he would ever hurt me, but the fact was, he did."

Before Diesel could respond, there was a knock on the door, and Cotton stepped into the room. "Well?"

Diesel looked over to him and said, "It's true. She's Ellie Blackwell."

Cotton raised his eyebrow. "Already knew that. Was hoping you could tell me something more."

"Wish I could, but she's not remembering everything yet. Just a few things here and there, and she can't remember anything about that night."

"Damn."

"If it's alright with you, I think we should hold off before we tell anyone that she's here."

"We've got some time, but not sure how much," Cotton told him. "We need to get down to that car and see if it's hers. Maybe there's something in there that might give us a better idea of what's going on."

Diesel stood up and started towards him. "I'm going with."

Cotton nodded, then looked over to me. "You sure that you can't remember anything about that night?"

"No. I really wish I could, but I can't. You have to know that I want to know even more so than you do."

"I know, and don't you worry. We'll get this thing figured out," he assured me.

"I'm really sorry about all this. I really didn't mean to bring trouble to your doorstep."

"Not worried about a little trouble. Hell, trouble is my middle name," he scoffed.

I had no idea why this man and his club had taken on my problems as their own, but I would forever be indebted to him—to all of them. "Thank you, Cotton."

He nodded, and Diesel followed him as he walked out of the room. When they closed the door behind them, I suddenly felt like I'd been tossed into the middle of the ocean, and without Diesel there, my only life preserver had been yanked away. I was treading water, trying to keep my head above as the waves of doubt and despair crashed down around me, and I was drowning in it. I tucked my knees under my chin and wrapped my arms tightly around my legs, trying to keep myself from falling apart. I'm not sure how long I stayed like that. I vaguely remembered Cassidy and Doc stopping by to check on me, but seeing that I needed some time alone, neither of them stayed long.

I spent the entire day in that room alone, wondering about what they might find in that car, and it was well after dark before they came rolling back to the clubhouse. I could hear them talking in the hallway, and I kept expecting Diesel to come to my room, but he didn't, at least not right away. It was another half hour before I heard a knock at my door, and by then, I was a nervous wreck. Relief washed over me when Diesel stepped into the room. For the first time since he'd gone, I felt like I could breath. As he walked over to me, I noticed that he had a large envelope in one hand and a purse in the other. I knew from the minute I saw it, it was mine, but I had to ask anyway, "Did you find that in the car?"

"We did."

"So, the car was mine."

"It was." As he handed me the purse, he took a step back and crossed his arms as he leaned against the dresser. He shook his head and sighed as he said, "You should've seen it. That car was smashed all to hell. It's a wonder how you made it out of there in one piece."

"I guess I really was *lucky* after all," I mumbled.

"Luckier than you may think." He held up the envelope as he said, "We found this in the backseat."

"What is it?" I asked as I opened it.

"Your divorce papers. Looks like you're no longer Mrs. Blackwell."

"What? They're signed?"

"Yep. All the i's have been dotted and all the t's have been crossed."

I'd had the papers drawn up years ago, but when I gave them to Brady, he told me that he'd kill me before he'd ever agree to a divorce. I tried many times over the years to get him to sign them, but he'd always refused, so I was more than a little surprised to hear that he'd finally done it. I quickly skimmed through the pages, and I was shocked to see that Diesel was right. "But how can that be?"

A concerned look crossed his face. "What do

you mean?"

"I don't remember him signing these." As I held the papers in my hand, an uneasy feeling washed over me, and goosebumps suddenly prickled against my skin, like someone had just walked over my grave.

"I know it's a lot to take in, but there's nothing worse than being stuck in a place where you don't belong. No matter how it all played out, those papers are your ticket out. You're free."

He was right. I'd spent years praying for the day when he would finally sign them, and now that he had, I could finally have the life that I'd always wanted—a life that didn't include him. I gave Diesel a small, yet uneasy, smile. "Okay ... I'm free. Now, what?"

"Now, we're going to see what Big can find out."

"He's the computer guy, right?"

"Yeah. He has a way of finding out things that nobody else can." He reached over and took the papers from my hand, placing them on the dresser behind him. "And while he's doing that, you and I are going to grab a bite to eat and watch a movie on TV. I figure you could use a break."

I'd felt like my life was spiraling out of control, and just like that, Diesel made it seem like everything was going to be okay. Like always, he had a way of knowing exactly what I needed. As he smiled at me from across the room, I found myself looking at him with wonder. I don't know exactly how or when it happened, but I'd grown feelings for him—strong feelings that filled my stomach with butterflies whenever I was around him. He was handsome—my God he was so handsome—but it was his heart, the kindness in his eyes, and the soothing sound of his voice, that I found so attractive. It was all those things that pulled me towards him like a magnet, and when I couldn't resist it a moment longer, I got up from the bed and walked over to him. My eyes drifted up to his perfect, full lips, and just thinking about kissing him had my entire body humming with anticipation. I needed to touch him, even if it was just for a moment, and from the way he was looking at me, I could tell he felt the same way. "Diesel?"

Electricity crackled around the room as his eyes locked on mine. "Um- hmm?"

"I'm not sure if this is a good idea ... you and me, but it just feels so right when I'm with you."

"It does feel right. In fact, I've never felt anything more right." He brought his hands up to my face, gently running the pad of one of his thumbs across my cheek as he looked down at me with those piercing, green eyes. Everything around me faded away, and in this moment, all my worries were forgotten as I listened to him say, "Angel, you've got me all tangled up inside. Hell, I don't know if I'm coming or going anymore."

He stood there just staring at me; the onslaught of emotions raging in his eyes stole my breath. My heart skipped a beat when he leaned over and covered my mouth with his in a hungry kiss. It was just me and him, and it was the most incredible feeling I'd ever experienced. The scent of his cologne. The feel of his body next to mine. The soft touch of his lips. It was everything I'd dreamed of and more. His hands dropped to my waist, and a small, needful moan vibrated through my chest as he pulled me closer. The caress of his lips was magic, making me feel like I was floating on air, and even though I feared that I might not ever have this chance again, I knew it couldn't continue. When he deepened the kiss, sending my need for him to a whole new level, I slowly brought my hands up to his chest and took a step back, breaking free from our embrace. We both stood there gazing at one another, not a word was spoken; we knew exactly what that kiss had meant. The feelings we'd been experiencing were mutual, and as much as we wanted to act on them, they would have to wait—at least for now.

Diesel leaned in towards me, kissing me lightly on the forehead. "How about that movie?"

"A movie sounds great."

"Great. You find something to watch, and I'll go throw a pizza in the oven."

When he turned to leave, I called out to him, "Diesel?"

"Yeah?"

"Thank you … for *everything*."

"There's something you should know about me, Lucky." His eyes grew intense as he said, "There's nothing I wouldn't do for the people I care about. So, as long as you'll let me, I'll be here for anything you need. And I mean it when I say *anything*."

With that, he walked out of the room.

While he cooked our pizza, I searched for a movie to watch. We spent the next few hours quietly enjoying each other's company, and by the time the movie was over, we were both exhausted. As I curled up in the covers of my bed, I asked, "Will you stay … for just a little longer?"

He nodded as he got up and took everything out of his pockets. After he placed everything on the dresser, he settled in next to me as my entire body started to relax. While I prayed it wouldn't happen, I had an aching suspicion that it was only a matter of time before I no longer had him by my side. My heart sank at the thought, and I found myself inching closer to him. It was like he could read my mind when he lifted his arm and waited as I nestled into his side. As soon as I laid my head down on his chest, he placed his hand on my shoulder and gently trailed his fingers down my arm as I closed my eyes and drifted off to sleep.

It wasn't long before I was being pulled into a place where I didn't want to be. I was back in my house, the new house that Brady had bought without even telling me —just like the new car and all his new, fancy clothes. My entire body filled with anxiety when I heard his voice booming through the darkness. Suddenly he appeared before me, and the hatred in his eyes sent chills running down my spine. At first, I couldn't make out what he was saying. His words were slurred, making it difficult for me to understand exactly why he was so angry, but then I noticed the papers in my hand and everything became clear.

"Get it through your thick fucking head. I'm not signing those goddamn papers!"

"I know what you've been doing, Brady." My back stiffened, and then I did something I hadn't done in years. I looked him right in the eye and said, *I saw you. I know everything.*"

"You don't know shit," he barked. "I haven't been doing a goddamn thing but working my ass off to put food on *your* table and a roof over *your* head."

"For the longest time, I couldn't figure out where all the money was coming from. I thought you might've gotten a promotion or borrowed money from your father, but I never dreamed you'd do something like this."

He took a charging step towards me, but I didn't back down. I held my head up and forced myself to look at him as he shouted, "You better think long and hard before you go down this road with me."

"Oh, I've thought about it. In fact, it's all I've been able to think about since those men showed up at the house. They were asking for you, and I gotta say, I got the feeling they were pretty ticked off about something. The funny thing about that little visit … it happened just a few days after I found those drugs and all that money in the crawl space upstairs."

I'd gotten his attention, and he was utterly speechless as he stood there glaring at me. Using his silence as an opportunity, I continued. "You know, I followed you to work, only you didn't go to the station. Instead, you went to some alley to meet some guy in a blue van."

Gathering his wits, he rolled his eyes and grumbled, "You are so fucking stupid. I'm working undercover."

"I thought of that, but you and I both know there's no way they'd let *you*, of all people, have those kinds of drugs and all that money here at the house."

"You don't know shit."

"Oh, really. Well, make a call down to the station. Get Michael on the phone so he can confirm what you've been saying." When he didn't move, I snickered, "That's what I thought.

The vein in his neck pulsed with rage as he clenched his fists at his side. "So, now what?"

"Brady, I don't care about your illegal dealings with these men. I truly could care less. I just want a divorce. That's it. All you have to do is sign these papers, and all will be forgotten. I'll walk out that door, and you'll never hear from me again."

"You think you've got it all figured out, don't you?" With an angry glare, he cocked his head to the side and asked, "What's to keep me from just killing you right here and right now?"

He had a point, and I didn't do a very good job at hiding it. When he saw the doubt flash through my eyes, he reached for me. Panic set in, and as I tried to fight him off, I stumbled. When my hip collided with the side of the table, I heard a familiar clank of metal knock against the hard glass. Hope surged through me as I turned to look down at the table and spotted his gun. With his hands already around my neck, I reached for it, flipping the safety before I pointed it directly at his temple. "Brady, don't."

He didn't move as he mocked, "What are you going to do? Shoot me?"

"Why wouldn't I?" I pulled the trigger back as I continued, "Don't you remember … I just found illegal drugs and unmarked cash in my house. Now, it's not *your* word against mine. Now, I have proof of the kind of man you are, and when I start talking, you better believe that everyone is gonna listen, including *your father*."

"No one will believe you, especially him," he snarled.

"Oh, he'll believe me. They all will, and there's nothing your father will be able to do about it. Not this time. This is too big for even him." I had no idea where I'd mustered up this newfound courage, but I used every ounce of it as I continued to point the gun directly at him. "So, it looks like you have two choices: You can either sign those papers and let me walk out of here, or you can spend the next twenty to thirty years in prison. What's it going to be?"

With a look of defeat, he lowered his hands from my throat and said, "If I sign these, how can I trust you to keep your word? How do I know you won't say anything?"

"Unlike you, I've never lied to you, Brady." As I offered him the papers, I said, "I give you my word that it will all be over as soon as you sign on the dotted line."

He snatched them from my hand, and without reading what was written inside, he flipped to the last page and signed his name. As he tossed them down on the table, he snarled, "There. It's done."

Maybe I was feeling overly confident, because I truly thought it was over as I reached for the papers. I'd only taken my eyes off of him for a second, and he used that as his opportunity to lunge towards me as he grabbed me tightly. The safety was off, and my finger was still on the trigger, so when I tried to jerk free from his grasp, the gun went off with an unforgettable pop. I watched in shock as he went sailing backwards, hitting the floor with a loud thud. An all-consuming fear engulfed me, and with my heart pounding against my chest, I woke up with a strained gasp. I sat up in the bed, trying to catch my breath as my eyes skirted around the room. Even though I knew I was no longer back at the house, the memory was still fresh in my mind like it had just happened, and I found myself staring down at my hand. I could almost feel the cold, hard metal of his gun pressing against my palm, and that's when I knew it wasn't just a dream.

I'd killed him.

Oh my God. I'd killed him

DIESEL

I'd fallen for Ellie Blackwell.

It didn't just happen, and it wasn't by some fluke or accident. No, my eyes were fucking wide open when I fell for her. Maybe I should've made more of an effort to avoid her, or kept my guard up, but I never stood a choice. She made me feel things I'd never felt before—good things, *really fucking good things*—and there was no way in hell I'd walk away from that. Some might say that I'd be a fool to get wrapped up in a girl with so many unknowns surrounding her past, but in my gut, I knew she was *the one*. I'd be naïve to think it'd be easy, but I didn't care what kind or how many obstacles stood in my way, I was going to make her mine. One way or another, Ellie's past would have to be dealt with, and I would be there, right by her side, and we'd face it head on —together.

Obviously, Ellie and I weren't thinking along the same lines, because when I woke up the next morning, I found myself alone in her bed with only a note that was left on her pillow. I broke out in a cold sweat as soon as I read the first sentence. It told me everything I needed to know. *Ellie was gone.* Fuck.

She'd taken my keys to the truck from the dresser, and since Drake and the others thought she was with me, they wouldn't have been watching the door. I had no idea what time of night she left, but since it was my truck she was driving, I doubted whoever was at the gate would've thought to stop her. Clutching her letter in my hand, I rushed out of bed and went to find Cotton. I was on my way to his office but heard his voice coming from the bar. When I walked in, I found him talking to Maverick. I was hanging on by a thread as I hurried over to them and handed Cotton the note. "I fucked up."

Cotton's eyebrows furrowed as he asked, "What's this?"

He didn't wait for my response. His eyes roamed over the words on the paper, and once he was done, he ran his hand roughly down his goatee and grumbled something incoherently under his breath. Noting his expression, Maverick peered over Cotton's shoulder and asked, "What's going on?"

With his focus still on the note, Cotton replied, "Ellie has gone and turned herself in to the cops."

"For what?"

I looked over to him and answered, "For killing her husband."

Maverick's eyes grew wide. "What the fuck? The chick on the news didn't say anything about murder."

"I'm just as clueless as you are," I told him.

"How long has she been gone?" Cotton asked.

"Got no idea." My stomach churned with guilt. It was

my job to keep an eye on her, and I'd gotten lax, thinking that as long as she was there with me, she'd be safe. "She slipped out while I was sleeping."

"If she wanted to leave, who are we to stop her?" Maverick shrugged.

Every muscle in my body tensed as I said, "She means something to me, brother, and I'm not gonna just let her walk away because she's got it in her head that she's brought trouble to the club."

Cotton gave Maverick a knowing look as he told him, "I'd think you'd understand. I seem to remember when Henley—"

"*That was different*," Maverick argued.

"Was it? I think I remember *exactly* how it was," Cotton mocked.

"I gotta do something," I interrupted. Just the thought of her facing the cops alone made my chest tighten. I could only imagine how scared she was, so I told them both, "I need to get down there ... I gotta be with her."

"Hold up. We don't even know where she is. I'll call Smoke and see if MJ can help." MJ, Smokey's ol' lady, was a lawyer and a good one at that. I've heard quite a few stories about the cases she'd won over the past year alone, and even though she was pregnant and spending most of her time at Smokey's orchard, it was clear that she had a knack for the law. She knew how to play the game, and I just hoped she'd be able to do something to help Ellie. As Cotton reached in his back pocket for his phone, he said, "Maybe she or somebody down at her firm can find out what the hell is going on."

"Good idea. I'll go see if Big has found anything we can use." Before I walked out of the bar, I turned to Cotton and said, "I appreciate you having my back on this, brother."

He nodded as he brought the phone up to his ear. While he talked with Smokey, I headed down the hall to find Big. When I got to his room, he was sitting at his desk working on his computer. "Have you found anything?"

"Yeah, you could say that," he said and glanced over his shoulder. "Damn, this Brady Blackwell guy is a real piece of work."

"You ready to share? Cotton and Maverick are back at the bar."

With a quick nod, he grabbed the papers from his desk and followed me down the hall. I was anxious to see what he might've uncovered, but I was more concerned about Ellie. When I asked Cotton if he'd heard anything new, he just shook his head.

"Going to take some time, but MJ's on it. She'll get back to us when she knows something."

"What's all that?" Maverick asked, noticing the stack of papers in Big's hand.

"Everything I could find on Officer Brady Blackwell."

"Well? Whatcha got?"

"Remember how the chick on the news said that he was a police chief's son? Well, that's about the only decent thing about him. Turns out, he's quite the fuck up." He laid the stack of papers in front of Cotton as he continued, "Apparently, our boy, Brady, has got a bit of a problem with anger management. He's got a shit-ton of write-ups for being over-aggressive during arrests as well as some written complaints by his fellow officers."

"Well, that comes as no surprise," Cotton scoffed.

"And we all know it wasn't just at work." He pulled several pages from the stack as he went on, "Things at home were just as bad, if not worse. There are pages and pages of reports where the cops were called to their house for domestic disturbances, and several of them match up with the dates that Ellie was admitted into the hospital. Crazy thing is, none of these reports were ever filed, and no charges were ever pressed."

"I'm guessing his father had something to do with that. Fuck. Ellie didn't stand a chance with this guy," Cotton growled. "Anything else."

"Turns out that IA has been looking into him."

"For what?"

"Missing evidence. False reports. You name it. He's gotten himself into a mess that not even his good ol' dad can get him out of." Big snickered.

Just as he finished talking, Cotton's phone rang. After checking the screen, he quickly answered, "What did you find out?" The room fell silent as we all listened when he asked, "How long is that gonna take?" He lowered his head and nodded silently as the person on the other end of the line spoke. "Let me know as soon as you find out what they're gonna do."

Right after he hung up the phone, he turned to me and said, "That was MJ."

"What did she say?"

"Ellie made it down to the station a couple of hours ago. The police are still questioning her. MJ is on her way down there to see what she can do to help."

"Do you think they'll arrest her?"

"She just confessed to murder. Doubt they're just gonna let her walk out of there," Cotton answered.

"So, now what?"

Cotton stood up as he replied, "Go get changed. You and I are gonna head down there and see if there's anything that we can do on our end."

In no time, we were on the road headed to the Lakewood Police Department where Ellie had turned herself in. The two and half hour drive was absolute torture. I couldn't stop imagining the worst, and it didn't help matters that we'd heard nothing back from MJ. By the time we finally pulled into the station's parking lot, I was ready to lose it. I tried to keep it together as I followed Cotton inside. As soon as we walked through the door, I spotted Ellie talking to a man in a suit. She was wearing one of my long-sleeved t-shirts with a pair of jeans, and her hair was brushed to the side, making it hard to believe that she was capable of murder. I started towards her and ignored Cotton as he warned me to stay put. When I approached them, Ellie looked up at me with wide eyes.

"What are you doing here?"

Her gorgeous, brown eyes locked on mine, and I could feel it all the way to my fucking toes. Just being close to her made it hard to think, and it took all I had not to grab her up and take her the hell out of there. I tried to keep my voice calm and reassuring. "Where else would I be?"

"I don't know." Her eyes immediately dropped to the ground. "I guess I figured you'd hate me after you found out what I did."

"That could never happen, Ellie. *Never.*"

"I appreciate you coming and everything, but you don't have to stay. I'm okay."

A flash of hope crossed her eyes as I told her, "I'm not

leaving until this thing is done. I meant it when I said I wasn't going anywhere."

The suit glared at me with disapproval and asked, "Is there something going on here that I should know about?"

"Um ... No. He's just a friend," Ellie answered. "He has nothing to do with any of this."

"If you say so," the asshole grumbled. A worrisome look crossed over her face when he added, "Let's continue this in my office."

Before she walked away, she looked up at me and whispered, "Thank you."

Once she was gone, I turned to find Cotton standing with MJ. She was talking on her phone while she paced back and forth with a frustrated expression on her face. With the amount of times I've been in MJ's company, never once had I seen her look so professional. Even in her highly pregnant state, she looked pretty damn impressive with her business attire and her hair pulled up in a tight bun.

When she saw us walking in her direction, she held up her finger, letting us know that she needed a minute. Seconds later, she hung up the phone and turned her attention to us. "The DA decided to press charges."

"So, what does that mean?"

"When Ellie and Brady were reported missing, the police went to the house. They found no evidence of a struggle, and without a body, anything they uncover at this point would be considered circumstantial. It would be a tough case to win, but because of who he is, they've decided to pursue."

"Damn."

"I know, but there's not a lot we can do at this point.

She confessed to killing a police officer. That's really all a judge needs to know."

"But people confess to things they haven't done all the time. It can't be that easy," Cotton argued.

"Yeah, but those people don't go missing for weeks. And you've also got to remember who Brady's father is. There's a lot that goes into play with all this," MJ reminded him. "I'm doing my best to get a hearing set up as soon as possible. If we can get a reasonable bail set, then she should be released in a few days."

"A few days? You mean she's gonna have to stay here?"

"It depends on the date that's set for her hearing. I'll do my best to get her out of here as soon as I can."

"When can I see her?"

"I'm not sure."

MJ barely had a chance to answer my first question when I impatiently hit her with more. "Have you gotten a chance to talk to her? Is she okay?"

"Yes, but only briefly. Ellie knows I'm here, and even though she wasn't exactly happy about it, she knows you sent me." She glanced down at her watch and said, "I need to get back in there. Stay close. I should know something fairly soon."

Once she'd turned and walked away, Cotton looked over to me and said, "Since it's gonna be a while, why don't we go grab a cup of coffee and a bite to eat. I saw a diner across the street."

"But—"

"Listen, I got no idea how this thing is gonna go, but you're no good to her like this, brother. You need to take a minute and pull your shit together before you see her."

Cotton was right, I really needed to focus on something else, even if only for the time being, so I followed him across the street. We were seated in a booth, and a waitress came over and took our orders. I drank my cup of coffee but barely managed to finish half of my scrambled eggs, bacon, and toast. My stomach couldn't handle much more. As I sat there staring out the window, it occurred to me how fast Ellie was becoming such an important part of my life even though I hadn't known her all that long. It was crazy, really. In truth, it shouldn't faze me if I ever saw her again, but it did—more than I even realized. Another thought crossed my mind as I played with my cold eggs— the weight of it overwhelming me to a point where I thought I'd crumble right on the spot—when I started to wonder if I could truly face the possibility of losing her.

"Are you done?" Cotton asked.

His voice pulled me from my thoughts, but I hadn't heard a word he'd said. "What?"

"Are you *done*?" Cotton repeated as he finished off his coffee. "Or do you need some more time to study that light pole out there?"

"I can't stop thinking about her," I answered as I leaned back in my seat. "This whole thing is fucking with my head."

"I get that you're worried about her, but she's stronger than you may think. You've gotta remember, she's been through all kinds of hell … The kind of hell that would crush most people, but she's still fighting. She's facing this thing head on, knowing that the odds are against her. You gotta give her credit for that."

"And what if I lose her in all this?"

"You just gotta have faith that you won't. You gotta be willing to fight just like she is," he explained.

"You're right. We'll find a way to get through this."

"Yes, *you will.*" He sighed, then said, "I know the timing sucks, brother, but we've got the run tonight. Gus already called to confirm, so you and the others will be leaving for Salt Lake at midnight."

Damn. With everything that had been going on with Ellie, I hadn't even thought about the run. Cotton was right. The timing sucked, but there wasn't anything I could do about it. The club came first. The men of Satan's Fury were my brothers, and after all they'd done for me, there was no way in hell I would ever let them down. Before I started prospecting for them, I was living in a shit-hole apartment and barely had two dimes to rub together. Now, I had a house of my own, a job at the shop, money in my pocket, and most of all, I had a family I could count on. Thankfully, this time we wouldn't be going all the way to Memphis. Since Clutch had secured the pipeline, we'd only need to make our trek to Salt Lake, drop off our delivery with the chapter there, and they'd deliver to the next drop off point. The entire shipment would make it to Memphis by the end of the week. "I'll be ready."

"I knew you would be. If everything goes as planned, you should be back before the hearing. You and I both know MJ will do everything she can to make sure everything goes without a hitch."

"God, I hope so."

"Let's get back over there and see what we can find out."

ELLIE

I've had a lot of surprises in my life, both good and bad, but not once had I ever imagined that I would find myself in jail. It wasn't like I hadn't expected it after I walked up to the counter and told the officer that I was Ellie Blackwell, and I'd murdered my husband, Brady Blackwell. The look on his face said it all. He was just as surprised at hearing the words as I was at saying them. After twelve hours of answering questions, being processed, and questioned again, I found myself behind bars. Needless to say, by the time I was done, I was completely drained. Exhausted beyond belief, I just wanted to sleep, but I couldn't. The mattress was hard and smelled foul—like a mix of body odor and vomit, and every time I closed my eyes, I heard strange noises or someone's voice bellowing from down the hall. I was terrified—panic-stricken, in a cold sweat—*terrified*, and as I lay there in the darkness night after night, I found myself wishing Diesel was with me. I'd managed to keep it together, at least for the most part, but as I continued thinking about him, I broke down and started to cry, and I just couldn't stop. I would've given anything for just one more night with him: to feel the warmth of his body close to mine, to hear the soothing sound of his voice, and to smell the intoxicating scent of his cologne.

Some say that bad memories hurt the most, but for me, it was always the good ones. Even though the time I shared with Diesel was short, those were the memories that'd be the most painful. They'd be a constant reminder of what I no longer had—what I might never have again. I stared at nothing and thought about the things that had happened in my life; however big or small or good or bad, I finally realized just how much each one of them had impacted my life. All those moments had left their mark and made me the person I was today. I had my regrets— more than I could count. I should've been stronger and done things differently. I should've found a way to break free from Brady, but I'd let myself believe that I was trapped. I'd convinced myself that I had nowhere to go because I had no family or friends who I could turn to and that I had no money. I let myself believe that I had no choice, but deep down, I knew that wasn't true. There was always a way, but I was too weak and simply too scared to run away from him. Now, because of the choices I'd made, I might never get the freedom I'd always dreamed of, and I'd lose the one person who was quickly becoming every-thing to me. I'd lose Diesel.

Considering the fact that I'd not only killed a cop, but I'd killed a police chief's son, I would've thought that I didn't stand a chance, but then I met MJ. After talking to her several times, I couldn't help but be impressed, and I knew she would do everything in her power to get me out of jail. The preliminary hearing was quickly approaching, and MJ had come once again to ask about what had happened that night. While she'd read that confession, she still felt that there was something missing. The guard led me down the hall and into an interview room; much like my cell, it was cold with white concrete walls. From the moment I walked into the station, I hadn't been able to get warm. I was cold all the way down to my bones, and with my overactive nerves, I couldn't stop trembling as I listened to MJ ask, "What happened after you shot him?"

"I grabbed my things and ran."

"Are you sure he's dead?"

That was the question I'd asked myself many times, and yet, I still didn't know the answer. "I'm ... I'm not sure. I think so. He wasn't moving and there was a lot of blood ... so I assumed—"

"And you didn't try to clean it up?"

"No. I just had to get out of there. I guess a part of me was afraid that he was still alive, and I wasn't going to take the chance on him coming after me again."

"What did you do with the gun? Did you take it with you?" she asked.

I thought back to that moment, remembering the panic I felt when the gun had gone off, and the loud clank it made when it hit the floor. "I didn't take it. I was so surprised that the gun had gone off that I dropped it on the floor. I know I had it pointed at him, and I'd threatened him with it, but I never intended to shoot him. But when he came after me ..."

"I know, Ellie. I know it wasn't the way you'd hoped it would play out, but he didn't give you a choice. You shot him in self-defense. We've just got to prove it." She wrote something down on her legal pad and then looked up at me and asked, "If you didn't take the gun with you, do you have any idea where it could be?"

"I honestly have no idea." I took a deep breath and asked her the question that had been weighing on my mind since my arrest. "If the gun is missing and Brady is nowhere to be found, does that mean he's alive somewhere out there?"

"I don't know, but I intend to find out." She assured me then leaned across the table and whispered, "If he's out there, I guarantee you the guys will find him. I'm sure as hell not letting you go to jail for a crime you didn't commit."

"I really appreciate you doing all this for me."

"You can stop thanking me, Ellie. I'm here because I want to be, and besides, it's not like Diesel would have it any other way." She teased, "It seems he's got a soft spot for you."

"I might have one for him myself."

"No," she replied sarcastically. "I would've never have guessed that."

"All the guys have been great, but there's something special about Diesel." I swallowed hard, trying to bite back my tears. "I've never met anyone like Diesel. I don't know what I would've done without him."

"You know, the men of Satan's Fury have a knack for that."

"For what?"

"Making you fall for them when you least expect it. I think there must be something in their water." She giggled.

"It must be something. After everything that's

happened with Brady, my mind tells me to steer clear of all men, that it just isn't worth the risk, but my heart ... my heart tells me that I can trust Diesel and the feelings I have for him. That's he's the kind of man who would put my happiness before his own, and he'd never hurt me."

"Seems like you know Diesel better than you think." She smiled. "Did he tell you about everything that happened with Zoe and their father's club?"

"He did."

"Then, you already know what kind of man he is." She cocked her head to the side. "He's proven that he'd put his neck on the line for someone he cares about, and I have no doubt he will do it again."

"So, maybe I'm not too crazy after all?"

"No. Not at all." She looked at me with apprehension as she said, "I'm not sure if you know this, but the guys are leaving tonight. They have some business to tend to in Salt Lake."

"What kind of business?"

With concern in her voice, she asked, "Has Diesel told you anything about the club?"

"Some, but I get the feeling that I'll never really know everything there is to know."

"You're right. You won't. It's not always easy, but there's one thing that you have to learn to deal with if you are going to have a future with Diesel."

"What's that?"

"Club business is never discussed with anyone except the brothers. They only tell us what we have to know, and the rest is kept confidential." When she noticed the confused look on my face, she continued, "It's for our own safety, Ellie. You just have to trust him and know that he is doing everything he can for his family. And if things keep going like they are, that will include you as well."

"So, you're okay with the not knowing?"

"Not always, but at the end of the day, I love Smokey. I love him more than anything, and the club has been a blessing in our lives. We know that we always have them if we need them, and the rest has a way of falling into place," she explained. "One day you'll understand."

Diesel had already proven to me that he was someone I could trust and knowing every detail about the club wasn't going to change that. "I think I already do."

"Good, because Diesel is one of the good ones and it's obvious he cares a great deal about you."

"Do you think he will be back for the hearing?"

"If I know Diesel, he'll do everything in his power to be here. Now, let's get back at it. I want to make sure we're ready for whatever they throw at us." MJ glanced back down at her legal pad and thought for a moment. It was clear her focus was back on the case when she said, "Since there is no body, no gun, and no sign of Brady whatsoever, I'm going to press for the charges to be dropped from murder to assault with a deadly weapon"

"Uh ... Okay."

"This way, we can focus on the self-defense strategy."

From that moment on, everything happened so fast that I could hardly keep up. When it came time for the preliminary hearing, I was a nervous wreck. I'd spent three long days behind bars, and I was practically trembling as I walked into the courtroom. As the guard led me to my seat, I found myself searching for Diesel. There was no sign of him, but Cotton and several of the others were sitting in the back row. They looked quite intimidating sitting there with their leather cuts and fierce facial expressions; knowing they were there to support me gave me a sense of strength I didn't know was possible—but I couldn't help but wonder why Diesel wasn't there. I gave them all a quick smile as I made my way over to my seat. Just as I sat down, the back doors flew open, and Diesel came charging inside. Relief washed over me as he started walking in my direction. As he knelt down behind me, he whispered, "Hey."

I glanced over my shoulder and smiled when I saw his handsome face. "Hey. I was worried you weren't going to make it back in time."

"No way I was going to let that happen. You doing okay?"

"I'd be better if this whole thing was over," I confessed. "I'm really sorry about everything. If I had known—"

"Don't," he interrupted. "Just focus on what lies ahead and getting out of here. I'm right here with ya, every step of the way."

"You're pretty great, you know that?" He smiled at me then stood up to go back to his brothers. I was about to turn back around when I spotted Brady's father sitting in the middle of the crowd. Just like his son used to do, he was glaring at me with pure hatred, sending a cold chill down my spine. Doing my best to ignore him, I turned my attention to the front of the room.

The next half hour was a blur. MJ presented our case to the court, and after the prosecutor was done dragging me over the coals with his harsh tongue-lashing, they bantered back and forth among themselves, discussing future dates and sequestering evidence. And then the moment came—the judge set my bail. As soon as I heard the astronomically high number, my heart dropped, knowing there was no way on earth that I could pay it. With my thoughts preoccupied, I never even looked in Diesel's direction as the guard led me out of the room. Back at the station, I changed clothes and was returned to my cell, where I immediately lay down and started to cry. I had no idea how long I'd been there sobbing into my pillow when one of the guards came up to me and slid my door open.

"Your bail has been posted."

"What? By who?"

She shrugged and gave me a look of indifference. "Got no idea. You'll find out when you get discharged up front."

I was too confused to be excited as I followed her down the hall and upstairs to the discharging room. They handed me back my clothes, and once I'd changed, they took me to another window where I was given my other personal belongings and told to sign several papers. As I filled out the forms, I glanced around the room and saw no sign of Diesel or the others. Having no idea who would've set my bail, I was starting to become anxious, then I heard a voice I hadn't heard in almost eight years.

"Hello, Ellie."

I quickly turned and found my father standing behind me. I was completely stunned and barely managed to mutter, "Dad?"

He stood with his arms nervously at his side, and there was pain behind his eyes as he spoke, "Your mom and I saw you on the news. When we found out what was going on—"

"Why are you here?" I interrupted.

"We were in the court room."

He just stood there staring at me, and I had no idea what he was thinking. I'd thought of this moment a million times, that I would yell and scream and curse him for not being the father I'd needed him to be, but as I stood there looking back at him, I realized how much I truly missed him. I missed all of them, and the fact that he was here now gave me hope that I could have the chance to fix the rift that had grown between all of us. "You haven't answered my question. What are you doing here?"

"I'm here to help."

"But why now?"

"I know I've made a mess of things. It was a mistake to turn my back on you all those years ago, and if I could take it back, I would." Tears filled his eyes as he said, "I'm so very sorry, Ellie. I was wrong. I know it isn't right for me to ask, but please forgive me for being a stubborn, old fool?"

I could've made it harder on him, but my heart had taken all it could. Just wanting it all to be over, I told him, "It wasn't all your fault. I was just as stubborn. I should've listened to you, but that was a long time ago. You're here now and that's all that matters."

He reached for me and wrapped his arms around me, hugging me tightly. It almost felt too good to be true to have him close. "I've missed you, Ellie. More than you can imagine."

"I've missed you, too. All of you." With my head resting on his chest, I told him, "There's so much I have to tell you."

"And I want to hear it all. Every single word. I hate that I've missed so much of your life, but that's over now. Your mother and I both want to make things right," he told me as he clung to me.

I was still in his arms when Diesel walked in with Cotton and MJ. I could tell by the expressions on their faces that they were surprised to see me standing there. I took a step back, and as I released my father from our embrace, I motioned my hand over to them. "Dad, I have some people that I'd like you to meet."

After I'd finished making my introductions, MJ smiled and said, "We came to post your bail, but I guess your father beat us to it."

It suddenly dawned on me just what my father had really done. "How could you afford to post my bail?"

"That's not for you to worry about."

"*Dad.*"

"It's fine, Ellie. It was the least I could do." He turned towards the door as he said, "Your mother is back at the house. You're welcome to come stay with us if you'd like."

I glanced over at Diesel, seeing the longing in his eyes, and I knew there was only one place I wanted to be. "I really appreciate the offer, but I've got a place to stay. Maybe, I could come for a visit soon?"

"I'd like that. Your mother would, too."

I hugged him tightly once again. Only this time I savored the moment, smelling the familiar scent of his after-shave and feeling the comfort of his loving arms. "Thank you for coming. It really means a lot to me."

"I love you, El. Always will."

"I love you, too."

Once he was gone, Diesel started towards me. As soon as I was within reach, he grabbed me and hugged me tightly as I melted into his arms. "I guess I should've asked this sooner, but is it okay if I stay with you?"

"You're kidding, right?" He chuckled. "There was no way I was letting you leave here with anyone but me, so yeah, you can stay with me."

"I was hoping you might say that."

"You ready to get out of here?"

"Absolutely." I reached in my pocket and as I handed him his keys, I grimaced. "You might need these."

"Yeah. *About that.*" He cocked his eyebrow and scolded, "We're gonna have us a little talk about how things are gonna be from here on out, but that can wait. For now, let's get you home."

As he took my hand in his and led me towards the door, my heart swelled with hope; I'd found someone who was brave enough to enter my storm. While I prayed it didn't engulf us both, I was relieved and thankful that Diesel would be by my side, helping me face the uncertainty of what still waited ahead.

DIESEL

e'd only been driving for a short time when we both decided to stop and grab a bite to eat at some café right outside of town. Ellie started talking the minute we sat down, telling me everything from how her memory had come back to how hard it was to sleep in her cell. Poor thing hadn't had anyone to talk to for days, so it didn't surprise me that she had so much to say. The entire time she rambled on, I couldn't take my eyes off of her. It was like my mind was having a hard time believing that she was really free. So I sat there, quietly staring as I listened to every word. I knew the last few days had taken its toll on Ellie, and I was eager to get her home, so as soon as she finished eating, I asked, "Are you ready to head back?"

"Yes. I'm dying for a hot shower and a change of clothes."

"Okay, then, let's get rolling."

We jumped in the truck, and then hit the road. When we finally made it back to Port Angeles, I turned down an old side road, which sparked Ellie's curiosity. Knowing it wasn't the way to the clubhouse, she turned to me with a confused look and asked, "Where are we going?"

"My place," I answered nonchalantly. I'd decided early on that instead of going back to the clubhouse, I was taking her to my place. Maybe I was being selfish, but I wanted her all to myself. "It's just up the road a bit."

"Your place? I thought you lived at the clubhouse?"

"I stay there from time to time, but I don't live there." As I started down another side road, I told her, "I always wanted a place out by the water. The house isn't all that great, but the view is out of this world. I'd really like to show you, if you're up for it?"

"I'm definitely up for it. I can't wait to see it." She was completely silent as I drove up the long, gravel driveway. I watched her expression as she leaned towards the window to get a better look, and when she saw the old, yellow, craftsman-style bungalow, her eyes lit up. "Wow. It's really beautiful, Diesel."

"It needs a lot of work, and I *will* get to it one of these days," I assured her as I put the truck in park. "Come on. I'll show you inside."

As she followed me up the steps and into the house, I found myself becoming nervous that she might not like it, but as soon as I put the key in the door and opened it, I heard her gasp. She stepped inside and walked straight towards the long row of floor-to-ceiling windows, which lined the back of the house. "Did you do all this?"

"Yeah. I figured if I was gonna have my house by the water, I was gonna enjoy it, inside and out." I chuckled and added, "Besides, it's a good distraction from the second-hand furniture and lack of decorations."

"Your furniture is great, but you're right." Her lips curled into a mischievous smile as she looked around. "It could use a picture or two on the walls."

I pointed to a tiny, four by six photograph that I had hanging in the kitchen. "I've got pictures. See? That's one of my very first motorcycle."

She walked over to the picture and studied it for a minute. "Um ... Diesel, that's a moped. It's just like the one my brother used to have, except this one is missing the little wire basket on the front."

"What? You've gotta be shitting me." I smirked, knowing very well that it was, indeed, a moped. My step-father had given it to me when I turned twelve, and it was a gift that left a lasting impression. "That sweet ride right there is a Honda PA50 1978 Hobbit."

"Yeah. Well, I hate to break it to you, but that sweet ride is a *moped*." The light in her eyes danced as she laughed, making her even more irresistible. I could actually feel myself being pulled towards her as she continued, "But don't worry. I won't hold it against you."

"Good to know."

After she took a quick look around the kitchen, she went back into the living room and stood by the windows. As she stared out at the ocean, she said, "You were right. The view really is amazing."

"I'm glad you think so."

"With a view like this, you should have a porch or a little patio. I could see myself spending an entire day out there just looking out at the ocean, drinking my coffee and reading."

"I hadn't thought about that, but you're right. It would be cool."

"Be warned. If you build one, I might never leave." She teased.

"I'll keep that in mind."

I gave her the full tour, and as we stood by the bathroom door, she asked, "Do you mind if I take a shower?"

"No, not at all." I grabbed some towels and started the water for her. "I'll go see what I can find for you to wear."

After I gathered up some of my clothes for her, I went into the living room and started a fire. It was the first time I'd had a woman at my place, and I was feeling a little off-balance. I wanted everything to be perfect for her, but under the circumstances, I had to make the best of what I had. I lit a few candles, turned on the TV, and tried to be patient as I waited for her to finish up in the bathroom. When she finally walked into the living room, I had to bite back my smile the minute I saw how my t-shirt and sleep pants hung on her small frame. Her hair was still wet, and her cheeks were flushed from the hot shower. Ellie looked absolutely adorable as she padded over to the sofa and sat down beside me. "Thank you for the shower. I can't tell you how much better I feel."

"No problem. I'm sorry about the clothes. We'll get you something that actually fits tomorrow."

"That's okay." She gave me a slight shrug. "I really like wearing your stuff. It makes me feel ... um ... never mind."

"No way. You're not going to start something like that and not finish it. What were you going to say?"

"I was just going to say that wearing your shirts makes me feel close to you. I really wish I had one with me when I was in that cell. I might've been able to sleep if I did." She rolled her eyes at me. "Happy now?"

"Actually, I am. More than you know."

"Can I tell you something without you thinking I'm crazy?"

"You can tell me anything."

"I missed you ... *a lot*. Probably more than I should have."

"I missed you, too, Ellie.

"There's a chance, *a good chance*, that I'll be going back to jail. It scares me to think that I might spend the rest of my life behind bars, but the thing that scares me the most is losing you. I've already lost so much, and I just don't think I could take it." She looked up at me with confusion. "See? It doesn't make any sense. Why am I afraid to lose you when you're not even mine? It's crazy."

"I'll tell you what's crazy. I've only known you for a couple of weeks and you already mean more to me than anyone else. You're all I can think about ... all I want. So, yeah, I'm scared too ... scared of wanting something I can't have. But I can promise you this—you don't have to be afraid of losing me. I'm yours in every way that counts, and I'm not letting you go."

"So, do you think we're *both* crazy?"

"Maybe, but I don't care." I reached for her, pulling her closer as I pressed my lips against hers. My need for her burned deep, and just the feeling of having her in my arms was like pouring gasoline on a fire. I brought my hands to the nape of her neck, bringing her even closer, and a light moan vibrated through her chest as I delved deeper into her mouth. Her arms snaked around my neck, and as her fingers tangled in my hair, she inched closer, pressing her breasts against my chest. Fuck. There was no denying the attraction between us. Hell, I could feel it coursing through my veins whenever she was near, and over the past few days, that feeling had only grown stronger. Our hunger for one another quickly escalated, causing the kiss to become wild and heated. We were completely lost in one another, and I didn't want the moment to end.

When we finally came up for air, Ellie looked at me with lust-filled eyes and said, "I've never felt anything like this before. It's a little overwhelming."

After everything that she'd been through, the last thing I wanted to do was push her into something if she wasn't ready. "We don't have to rush into anything here. You're worth the wait."

With her eyes locked on mine, she stood up and extended her hand to me. "I don't want to wait, Diesel. I'm tired of waiting for what I really want, and I want this more than anything."

I took her hand and followed her into the bedroom. When we reached the foot of the bed, she reached for the hem of my shirt, and as she started to ease it over my head, she said, "I've thought about this moment so many times."

"I want you to be sure."

She tossed my shirt to the floor, then reached for her own and slowly lifted it over her head, exposing her perfect, round breasts. We both knew her scars were there in plain sight, but neither of us paid them any mind. It was just Ellie and me. "I've never been more sure."

The damn broke as soon as the words slipped from her mouth, and as she stood there staring at me with hunger in her eyes, all the heat and desire I had been holding back flooded over me. Every ounce of resistance had vanished, leaving me completely helpless to fight the urge to have her. Like a starved animal, I closed the gap between us, and a flash of desire crossed over her eyes as my hand dove into her hair. I grabbed the back of her neck as my lips crashed into hers, our tongues twisting and tasting each other with nothing but passion and desire. Her mouth was warm and soft, and each swirl of her tongue made the blood rush straight to my cock.

As I lowered my mouth to her neck, I whispered, "I'm going to erase all your bad memories, angel. Every damn one of them." I ran my lips leisurely from the curve of her jaw down to her shoulder. "You'll only be able to remember the feel of my mouth on your skin, my hands on your body, and the thrust of my cock when I bury myself deep inside you—over and over. Everything else will be forgotten."

"Yes," she rasped.

The feel of her body against mine sent me over the edge, and my hands suddenly became rough and impatient. I had to have her—all of her. I continued trailing kisses past her collar bone, and her fingers tangled in my hair, pulling me towards her as I lowered my mouth to her breast. Heavy breaths and low moans filled the room as I flicked my tongue against her nipple. Her head fell back, leaving no doubt that she liked having my mouth on her. With her eyes closed, she mumbled, "You have no idea how good that feels."

Goosebumps prickled across her skin as my fingers worked their way across her abdomen, through the waistband of her sleep pants, and further down between her legs. A small whimper escaped her throat as my fingers grazed across her center. Unable to contain herself, she rocked her hips forward, begging for my touch. Aiming to please, I slid my fingertips inside her and had just begun to stroke her when she moaned, "Oh god, Scotty ... Please, don't stop."

Hearing my name on her lips drove me wild, and as I brushed my thumb against her clit, I felt her begin to tremble. Knowing she was close, I worked two of my fingers deeper inside of her, finding her G-spot, and as I increased the pressure, her fingernails dug into my shoulders. Her breath quickened, and her head dropped forward as her entire body tensed with her release. I couldn't wait any longer to have her; I withdrew my fingers and moved my hands to her waist, reaching for the drawstring of her pants. As soon as I gave it a quick tug, they fell useless to the floor. Equally as eager, Ellie reached for mine, and in a matter of seconds, we were both completely undressed. The room stood silent as we each took a moment to gaze at one another; the sight of Ellie took my breath away. Like a dream, she was absolutely spectacular.

Without saying a word, she placed the palms of her hands on my chest and eased me back on the bed. As much as I didn't like giving up control, I could see the self-assurance in her eyes, and I wanted to keep it there— to have her feel strong and confident with me. When she started towards me like a hungry predator, I couldn't have desired her more. I reached for her hips, carefully lifting her as she straddled herself over my cock. Dragging her center across my throbbing erection, she leaned forward and kissed me passionately. I thought I'd lose my mind if I had to wait another minute to be inside her.

Feeling the same need burning inside of her, Ellie looked down at me and asked, "Do you have a condom?"

"Side table. Bottom drawer."

She reached into the drawer and handed me the small, square package; as soon as I slid it on, she was back, centering herself on top of me. The heat of our breaths mingled between us until the anticipation became too much.

"I want you, Ellie. All of you." My hand snaked up her spine. "I've never wanted anything more."

My breath became strained as I tried to fight the temptation to take over. Noting my struggle, she lowered her hand between us and started stroking me. A fevered hiss slipped through Ellie's lips as she slowly inched down, taking me deep inside. She was so fucking tight and warm and wet that I thought I would explode right there on the spot. Ellie felt like heaven, absolute heaven; I wanted to savor every second, feel every sensation.

A deep growl resonated through my chest as she quickened her pace, and even though it felt incredible, I needed more. Unable to control myself, I brought my hands up to her hips and guided her up and down. Her nails dug into my chest as she bucked against me, meeting every thrust with more force, more intensity. "That's it, angel. Give me everything you've got."

Each drive became more frantic as she took me deeper and deeper. My body was wound tight as I struggled to hold back my climax, and I could feel the pressure building as her walls constricted around me. Teetering close to the edge, I dug my fingertips into her hips and held on as her orgasm approached. "Oh, God, Scotty."

"That's it, angel. Come for me." Her hips rocked against mine in a feverish rhythm until she let out a tortured groan. With one last, deep thrust, Ellie's body tensed, and her breath stilled as her head fell back. Her orgasm exploded as she clamped down around me, making it impossible for me to hold back as she continued to buck against me. The fire that raged within me reached its breaking point as I came deep inside her. "Fuck."

I held on to her hips, holding her in place as I caught my breath. Still trembling, Ellie collapsed on top of me, her heart beating wildly next to mine; neither of us moved as the aftershocks from our pleasure rolled over us. I ran my fingers through her hair and whispered, "You're absolutely incredible, Ellie. Everything I dreamed of and more."

We were both still trying to catch our breath when she said, "I didn't know … I never thought it could be like that."

"Baby, you haven't seen nothing yet."

ELLIE

I'd all but given up on finding happiness, deciding that it simply wasn't in the cards for me. I started to think that I was destined to live my life with tears in my eyes and an ache in my heart, but I was wrong—so very wrong. To my absolute wonder, I found someone who, without hesitation, has faced all the turmoil and doubt of my recent events, and given me everything he's got for support. He made everything seem easy, and that as long as he was by my side, I could handle anything. For the first time since I'd left home, he made me feel like I had a place where I belonged—that I belonged with *him*. I wanted to trust my feelings. I wanted to take a chance and hold on to the happiness that I've found with him, but the looming doubt of what was to come terrified me. It was impossible to think about the future when my past was holding us back, and that's when I realized that there was nothing worse than being stuck in a place where you didn't belong. I was going to take a chance. I was going to take a chance with Diesel and the life we could have together.

It wasn't exactly a difficult choice. He'd been wonderful to me from the start, and things just kept getting better. The next morning, I woke up to the sound of pots and pans banging in the kitchen. When I rolled over and found myself alone in the bed, I got up and threw on one of Diesel's old t-shirts. My feet were freezing, so I grabbed a pair of his socks and slipped them on, too. After I pulled my hair up in a ponytail, I went to see what Diesel was up to. As soon as he saw me heading towards him, a sexy smile crossed his face. "Good morning, beautiful."

"Morning." I smiled as I walked over to the stove. "What's all this?"

"Thought I'd make us up some breakfast." He leaned towards me and kissed me on the temple. "I hope I didn't wake you."

As I rubbed the sleep from my eyes, I asked, "What time is it?"

"Almost eleven."

"Eleven? I had no idea I'd slept that long." I watched as he cracked a few eggs into a bowl. "Can I help you do anything?"

"Nope. I've got it. Why don't you grab a cup of coffee and keep me company?"

After I poured myself a cup, I walked over to the end of the counter and sat down on one of the stools. My heart swelled as I watched him, the rough and tough biker, scurry around the kitchen like a professional chef. He never failed to surprise me, and I found myself wondering how I'd gotten to be so lucky. "Can I ask you something?"

"Anything you want. Unless it's the recipe for my biscuits. That's a secret." He teased.

"Why are you doing all this for me?"

"Well, it's not just for you." He smiled. "I plan on eating, too."

I sighed with a playful roll of my eyes. "That's not what I meant, and you know it."

"I don't know. Maybe I was just overcome with a need to help a damsel in distress."

"Seriously? That's all this is to you?"

An intense expression crossed his face as he laid the spatula down on the counter and walked over to me. "No, Ellie. That's not *all this is to me*. I wish I knew how to explain it, but I honestly don't even understand it myself. This thing … this connection between us baffles me, but I like it. I like it *a lot*."

"I like it, too."

"You're an amazing woman." He brought his hand up to my face, cupping my jaw as he continued, "Even after everything you've been through, there's still a fire burning in you. You haven't given up, and something tells me, you never will."

"So, what you're saying is … you like me?" I goaded.

His mouth dropped to mine as he kissed me tenderly, leaving me completely breathless. I'd barely had a chance to recover when he said, "Yeah, that's what I'm saying."

"Good." I replied with a smile. "Because I'm pretty crazy about you, too."

"I guess we're all set then." He smirked as he moved

back over to the stove. "Now, let me cook, woman. I'm starving."

After we ate, we bundled up in his clothes, and he took me for a stroll down by the water. We spent hours just walking and talking, and after we made our way back to his house, we spent the afternoon making love. It was wonderful, mainly because neither of us spoke about my case or the unknowns surrounding it, and it stayed like that for the next few days.

During one of those days, Diesel took me to the local drug store to pick up a few toiletries, and a cute, little boutique to buy a couple of items of clothing and under-garments, considering I'd left with nothing but the clothes on my back. Another day, we went to some of his favorite places: a little diner at the edge of town, a secret trail tucked away in the mountains, and a beautiful waterfall at Cape Flattery. I couldn't imagine a better way to spend a day. Each day we just took our time to enjoy one another's company—until one simple conversation changed everything.

It was early. The sun was just starting to come up, and as I stood there staring out the window, I marveled at just how beautiful it was. Without even realizing it, I let out a troubled sigh. Diesel came up behind me and offered me a cup of coffee. As I reached for it, he asked, "You got some-thing on your mind?"

"I was just thinking."

"Thinking about what?" He pushed.

"You."

His lips curled into a sexy smile. "What about me?"

"Why don't we just run away somewhere ... maybe one of those little islands by Fiji."

147

"Sounds pretty tempting."

I gave him a small smile. "Yes, it does, but we both know we can't do that."

"Unfortunately, you're right." He took a sip of his coffee as he looked out the window. "Can I ask you something?"

"Sure."

"There's something about that night that's been bothering me. I don't know what it is, but I thought it might help if we talked about it. Maybe we can figure it out together."

"Okay."

"You said that you asked him for a divorce. Was that the first time you'd asked him?"

"No. I'd asked him one time before." I sighed. "Honestly, our marriage was doomed before it even began. We were young and clueless, and neither of us were happy. After I lost the baby, it took months before I could even look at him, but I stayed because I had nowhere else to go. I was stupid enough to think he wouldn't hurt me again, but he did. You know, I kept thinking … if I was good to him and made him happy that he would stop. Eventually, I just shut down."

"So, what happened when you asked him for a divorce the first time?"

"He freaked out. I thought he'd be happy to get rid of me, but he refused. We had a huge argument, and I spent three days in the hospital. He told me if I tried to leave him, he would kill me. Needless to say, I wasn't exactly eager to ask him about it again."

"Damn. I really want to fucking kill this dude."

"I think it's a little late for that." I teased.

"For his sake, I hope it is," he grumbled.

"Brady wanted everyone to think that he had the perfect life, but the truth was, other than the fights, we hadn't touched each other in years. I got to the point where I just avoided him at all cost."

"So, what made you decide to ask him to sign the papers this time? Did something happen?"

"It's kind of a long story," I started. "I kind of black-mailed him."

"*Blackmailed* him?" His voice was filled with surprise. "With what?"

"These men came by the house ..."

His eyebrows furrowed. "Wait. What men?"

"I don't know. I'd never seen them before. They had on vests like you and the guys wear, only theirs had something different written on them."

"Fuck." He raked his fingers through his hair as he thought about what I'd just revealed. "Do you remember what it said?"

"Something Saints, but I'd have to think about it to remember the rest."

"Why did they come to your house?"

"They were looking for Brady. They kept asking all these questions about where he might be. They seemed pretty adamant about finding him." I sighed with frustration. "The whole thing was very odd."

"So, then what happened?"

"At first, nothing. I figured it had to do with some arrest he'd made or something like that, but then, I got to thinking about all the money he was suddenly making. It wasn't the kind of money from a police officer's salary, at least not that I know of, so I started searching for some kind of clue. I didn't really know what I was looking for, but after a couple of days, I finally found it."

"What did you find?"

"Drugs. At least that's what I thought it was. It was a duffle bag filled with white bags of powder, and there was also a big sack of money."

"Damn." His entire body grew tense as he crossed his arms and asked, "So, you used all that to blackmail him into signing the papers?"

"Yeah, but it didn't exactly go as planned. I think he got spooked after he signed the papers. He thought I might tell somebody what I'd found, so he came after me," I explained. "But at least I got all of it hidden before I left."

"Hold on." He stepped towards me. "You hid the money and the drugs?"

"Yes, and if he's alive out there, I bet he's pissed that it's not where he left it." I shrugged. "I figured I could use it as collateral after I got the papers signed. I'd tell him where I put it once I was off somewhere safe, but everything blew up in my face before I could tell him what I'd done."

"So, he has no idea that you have the duffle bag?"

"Well, I don't actually have it." I grimaced. "I just moved it."

"Where?"

"I really didn't have enough time to hide it away from the house, so I put it where the filter goes for the air conditioning unit. Do you know what I'm talking about?" When he nodded, I continued, "I opened it up and slid it under the house, where you couldn't see it."

"Damn. You're a smart one, Ellie Blackwell." He looked over at the clock, and even though it was early, he said, "I need to call Cotton. I want to see if he has any idea who might've come knocking at your door."

"Do you think it really matters? It's bad enough that I shot Brady, but if the judge finds out that I was blackmailing him, he'll think I had motive for killing him."

"When the judge finds out that Brady was up to no good, it's going to help you, not hurt you, angel. It's time for us to turn this thing around and prove once and for all what a piece of shit Officer Brady Blackwell really is."

I watched as he reached for his phone and called Cotton, telling him everything I'd shared with him. Apparently, his interest was piqued when he heard that another club might be involved, so he told Diesel to bring me over to the club. We both went to his room to get dressed, and as I looked to grab my things, I realized that I'd run out of clean clothes. Having no other choice, Diesel gave me some of his things to wear, and we were on our way. Once we were at the clubhouse, Diesel led me down a hallway I'd never been and right into Cotton's office. Cotton was talking to Maverick and Stitch when we walked in. After each of them quickly greeted us, Cotton turned to me and said, "Why don't you tell us what you can remember about the guys who came to your house?"

All eyes turned to me as they waited for my answer. I'd only met Stitch a couple of times, so I still wasn't used to his intense expression. Trying my best not to let it intimidate me, I told him, "There were four of them. They were riding motorcycles like yours, and they were wearing vests like the ones you wear."

"Diesel said you remembered seeing the word *Saints*

embroidered on their patch." He handed me a photograph and asked, "Did it look like this?"

I looked down at the picture of a man wearing a vest, and as soon as I saw the name *Forsaken Saints*, I knew it was them. "Yes. This looks exactly like the vest they were wearing. In fact, I think this was one of the guys who came to the house. Do you know them?"

He didn't answer. Instead he looked over to Stitch and said, "Put a call in to Rip. Tell him we'll be heading that way in a couple of hours."

Stitch nodded, then headed out the door. Once he was gone, Cotton turned his attention back to me. "Diesel said you'd hidden some drugs and money at your house. Do you think it's still there?"

"It should be, unless someone found it."

"Is there a way we can get in there without anyone seeing us?" he asked.

"It would be kind of hard, considering there are security cameras everywhere. I'm not sure how to get past them without being seen."

"We can take care of that, but once we're in, we're gonna need you to show us where you hid the drugs."

"Okay."

"And while we're there, maybe you can grab some of your things." His eyes skirted over me as he smiled and said, "You know, maybe some clothes that actually fit." Cotton apparently wasn't done with me yet when he added, "By the way, darlin', these *vests* right here"—he pointed his thumb at his chest and then swirled an index finger at Diesel's—"are called *cuts*. It'd do you well to remember that."

At least he still had a smile on his face when he said it.

While the idea of getting my things excited me, the thought of going back to that house did just the opposite. I hadn't been back there since the day I'd shot Brady, and I hadn't planned on ever going back, but I knew it was something I had to do, especially if Cotton asked. After all they'd done for me, there was no way I would tell him no. I listened as Cotton put a call in to Big.

"Need you to do something for me. See what you can do about the security cameras at Ellie's place ... Better yet, kill the power on the whole fucking street. I don't want to take any chances on anyone seeing us." After he paused for a moment, he continued, "I'll text you when we get there. Thanks, brother."

As soon as he hung up the phone, I followed the guys out to Cotton's SUV, and once we were all inside, he started driving towards my house. Almost three hours later, we were pulling into the alley behind my garage. After Stitch surveyed the area and gave us the signal that the coast was clear, I led the others through the back entrance and up to the side door of the house. Trying to hide my uncertainties, I used my key to unlock the door.

An eerie feeling washed over me as we walked inside. It was like a part of me expected Brady to be there waiting for me, ready to seek his revenge for what I'd done, and that feeling only got worse as I stepped into the kitchen. My eyes dropped to the floor where I'd left him, and I was surprised that there was no sign of blood anywhere in sight. In fact, the place was spotless, like the shooting had never happened. I looked around the room and noticed how the chairs sat perfectly around the table, the vase that had been knocked over was back in its place, and the rug that had always been in front of the stove was now missing. I was completely baffled. "This doesn't make any sense. This isn't how it looked when I left."

Diesel looked over to me and asked, "What do you mean?"

"Everything's been put back where it belongs, and Brady ..." I pointed to the floor. "That's where he was when I left."

With a blank expression, Cotton asked, "Where's the bedroom?

"Down the hall. The second door to your left."

I followed him into the bedroom and watched as he went straight to the closet and opened the door. "Do you notice anything missing?"

"His clothes are gone ... and our luggage, too." I gasped. "Does this mean he's still alive?"

"I'm not sure what it means. Take us to where you stashed the bag, and then quickly, go grab some of your things. We need to get the fuck out of here."

They all followed me down the hall, and after I showed them where I'd hidden the drugs and the money, I went back to my bedroom to get what I wanted of my things. My mind was reeling as I started shoving clothes and whatever else into my bag. I didn't even hear Diesel when he walked up behind me. "You okay?"

"Shit!" I gasped. "You scared me."

"I take that as a *no*." I reached for my bag and placed it on the bed, then he wrapped his arms around me and quietly hugged me. My pounding heart began to slow down as the tension in my muscles started to fade. After several seconds, he whispered, "It's gonna be okay, angel."

"Are you sure? I'm really starting to have my doubts about that," I confessed. "If he's alive, he's going to come looking for me. There's no way he's just going to let me walk away, especially after I shot him and took his bag."

"You let *me* worry about that. I'm not going to allow anything to happen to you." With a look of pure determination, he said, "No one will ever hurt you again."

"Diesel! We got everything." Cotton shouted from the hall. "We need to get rolling."

"Two minutes!" Diesel reached for my bag. "Grab whatever else you think you might need."

After I gathered up a few more of my things, we went to the kitchen to meet Cotton and Stitch. As soon as we did, Cotton asked, "Ready?"

Diesel nodded, and as we walked outside, I glanced back at my house and felt a sense of relief knowing that it was the last time I would ever walk through those doors. As I turned to leave, I realized that what I was moving towards was so much better than what I was leaving behind. It was time for me to let go of the past and put all the memories of Brady where they belonged—in the past. I just prayed my future would let me.

DIESEL

*J*learned a long time ago that having courage didn't mean you weren't scared. To help Ellie, I was ready to face whatever unknowns lay ahead, but that didn't mean I wasn't worried about how things might play out. None of us had any way of knowing how Brady was connected to the Forsaken Saints, or why they'd come looking for him, but Cotton was determined to find out. I wasn't exactly thrilled that we were taking Ellie with us, but time wasn't on our side. When I glanced over at Ellie, I could see she was nervous, so I reached for her hand, giving it a light squeeze. As we pulled up to the man who stood at the gate, Cotton rolled his window down and said, "Hey, Dive."

When he approached the SUV, I noticed he was wearing a *Sergeant at Arms* patch on his leather jacket. He brushed his long, shaggy hair out of his eyes as he said, "Cotton. Long time no see, brother."

"Same to you. How you doing these days?"

"Pretty good." He crossed his arms with an exaggerated shake. "I'd be doing better if it wasn't so fucking cold."

"You ain't lying. I'm ready for a break from all this fucking snow." Cotton looked towards the clubhouse and asked him, "Is Rip inside?"

"Yeah. He's been expecting you. Go on in. I'd come with, but I've gotta finish setting up this new security camera before Rip comes unglued."

"Good luck with that." Cotton laughed as he pulled forward. Once we were parked, I looked at Ellie and leaned over, feeling the tension radiating off of her. "You don't have to be nervous about going in there. These guys are friends of the club."

She slowly nodded and followed us inside. Their clubhouse was a lot like ours, rustic and full of character, but it was much smaller. I'd never officially met any of the Saints' brothers, but I knew we had history with them. Clutch once told me that they'd had our backs when Cotton's cousin tried to take down our club. It was a long time ago, but their help left a lasting impression with Cotton and the others. I hoped their connection would come to be useful when we questioned them about Brady Blackwell.

I could hear voices coming from the bar, but as soon as we walked in, the room grew quiet. One of the older guys stood from his seat, and his face grew red as he said, "Damn, Cotton. Why the fuck did you bring her here?"

"Easy there, Rip," Cotton warned. "We're not looking for trouble."

"I get that, but ... fuck." He ran his hand roughly through his beard and grumbled something under his breath. It was clear that he wasn't happy about Ellie being there, and it took him a minute to collect himself. Rip was the president of the Forsaken Saints, and from what I'd heard, he was a decent, but firm, man. His club was small, but he'd led them well and from the looks of it, their club was doing okay for itself. "Why you'd bring her here of all places? Hell, she's been all over the goddamn news."

"I'm fully aware of what's been going on with her, and that's why we're here. We were hoping you could tell us something about her husband, Brady Blackwell."

"What exactly were you wanting to know?"

"Anything you can tell us."

"I can tell you that he's a double-crossing piece of shit. What else do you want to know?"

"When was the last time you saw him alive?"

"There a reason you need to know?" Rip asked.

Cotton looked over to Ellie as he said, "You could say that we've taken her in as one of our own, and since you've seen the news, you know she's run into some trouble with the cops."

"Yeah, I know." He motioned Cotton forward. "Come with me."

When he started to walk out of the room, Cotton turned to Ellie and said, "Wait here."

Her eyes widened with trepidation, letting me know that she didn't like the idea, but she didn't try to argue. I walked over to her and said, "There's a table in the back corner. Just wait there, and I'll be back as soon as I can."

"Does this mean he's alive?"

"Not sure what it means, but I'm gonna find out."

"Okay."

As much as I hated the thought of leaving her, I knew Cotton wouldn't ask her to stay behind if he didn't think she'd be safe. I kissed her on the forehead and watched as she started towards the back of the room. When I went to join the others, the girl from behind the counter called out to me. "She'll be fine. I'll keep an eye on her."

"Thanks. I'd appreciate that."

By the time I caught up to Cotton and Stitch, they were going out the back door with Rip. I followed them through the parking lot and over to their garage. It was just like any other garage with its tools and old parts laying around along with a couple of older bikes they'd been working on. When Rip got to a door in the back of the room, he turned to Cotton and said, "Before we go in here, I should probably ask ... is this guy a friend of yours?"

"Fuck no," Cotton growled.

"Good to hear." Rip smirked as he opened the door and started down a short hall. With its dark lighting and putrid smell, it felt ominous to say the least. It didn't help matters that there wasn't any heat—it was just cold and damp, yet the others seemed unfazed by their surroundings as they headed forward. I had no idea what we were about to see when Rip finally made it to the last doorway. As he reached for the door handle, he looked back at us and said, "Just a forewarning, this ain't gonna be pretty."

Cotton nodded, and we all watched in silence as he eased the door open. The room looked like some prison cell in a third-world country. The walls were made of concrete, and they were stained with dried blood and God knows what else. There were no windows, so it was hard to make out the figure that was sitting over on the dirty, old cot until we stepped inside. When I finally saw him, I felt a sense of gratitude for the Forsaken brothers. Good, old Brady had finally gotten what he deserved. Hell, the guy looked like he was on his last leg. Both eyes were practically swollen shut, and his face looked like it had been used for a punching bag. Along with the bullet wound to his shoulder, he was covered in cuts and bruises, and his clothes were soaked in blood. And the motherfucker smelled like ass. Just being in the same room with him brought bile to my throat. As I stood there staring at him, I thought about everything he'd done to Ellie and had to fight the urge go over and finish him off.

When Brady saw us standing there, his shoulders drooped, and he lowered his head like a cowering dog. "I already told you … I don't know where the fuck it is. I don't know what else you want from me."

When Rip motioned his head towards the door, we all followed him back into the hall. Once he'd closed the door behind us, Cotton stepped towards him. "What's this all about? Why are you keeping him here?"

"The motherfucker is a double-crossing, lying, piece of shit, that's why," Rip growled. "The dickhead arrested one of our distributors a couple months back, but he didn't take him to jail. Turns out, he wasn't all that interested in finding justice. No. This fuck-wad was looking to make a quick dime. He took our shit and thought he could get away with it. Did some looking into the guy, and he's made a habit of doing this shit. But this time, he fucked with the wrong people. He's not leaving that room until my shipment and my cash are back in my hands."

Without mentioning that we had what they were looking for, Cotton said, "Did you have anything to do with the cleanup back at Ellie's place?"

"Yeah, but I had no way of knowing it would come

back on your girl." He crossed his arms and he leaned his shoulder against the wall. "Once she left, I figured she was gone for good. Had no way of knowing that she'd grow a fucking conscience and turn herself into the cops."

"So, you knew she bolted?"

He nodded. "I'd had Link, one of my boys, watching their house. Link had given us the word that Brady was there, and since he didn't show up at our meet and was dodging my calls, I decided it was time to pay him another visit. When we got there, the two of them were arguing about something. Damn. It was one hell of a fight, too. We only caught the tail end of it, but we heard enough to know that she was done with his shit. We thought it was over until he decided to go after her. Looked like he was about to kill her, and we were about to step in when she shot his sorry ass." He looked over at Cotton with a heartfelt expression. "I gotta tell ya. After she shot him, it scared the hell out of that poor girl. You should've seen the look on her face."

"From what I've seen, the whole thing has hit her pretty hard, but damn. That asshole had it coming. He'd put her through all kinds of hell."

"Figured that much. Got to be one huge fucking pussy to lay your hands on a woman. I was happy to see her stand up to him, and I couldn't leave there without helping her out," he confessed.

"What are you talking about?"

"I didn't want the cops to come looking for her, especially since the fucker wasn't dead, so we packed his shit and made it look like he'd left on his own free will."

"Damn. I never saw that one coming."

"That's why I was so surprised when she showed up

here," Rip explained. "Like I said before, when I saw her leave, I thought for sure she wouldn't be coming back."

"Things have a way of coming full circle, brother. This thing had to play itself out." Cotton ran his hand over his goatee as he cocked his eyebrow. "I'm gonna have to ask a favor, brother."

"Whatever you need."

"Just a minute to talk to him."

Rip reached for the door, and as he opened it, he said, "Take all the time you want."

Stitch and I followed Cotton inside, and when Brady saw us coming towards him, he tried to put on a brave front. "Who the fuck are you?"

"Damn. You really do suck. Figured you would've learned something from your old man, but it looks like you didn't learn shit. Hell, you can't even ask the right fucking question. What you should be asking is 'how bad do I want this shit to end?'" Cotton crouched down in front of him and said, "You've found yourself in one hell of a mess this time. Fucked with the wrong man, and he's a determined motherfucker. He's not gonna stop until he gets what he wants, but things are looking up. Seems that we've got the means to make all this shit end, but we're gonna need you to do something first."

"And how the hell are you gonna do that?" he grumbled. "Like you said, these motherfuckers aren't gonna stop until they get what they want, and I don't have it."

"Yeah. I got all that." Cotton snickered. "So, it's time to ask yourself ... how bad do you want this to be over?"

"Pretty fucking bad."

"In that case, it's time for you to listen, and if you have any good sense at all, you'll pay close attention, or these guys are gonna keep pounding away at you until there's nothing left."

"Just tell me what you want me to do," he pleaded.

"Need you to make a call to the chief … convince him to do whatever he's gotta do to get the charges against Ellie dropped."

His back stiffened as he barked, "Ellie? What are you talking about? What charges?"

"She's been charged with your murder."

"Wait. Let me get this straight." An evil grin spread across his face as he said, "Ellie has been charged with my murder, and you want me to help her get out of it? You gotta be kidding me? That fucking whore can rot in jail for all I care."

From the minute I'd laid eyes on the worthless piece of shit, I'd wanted to have my go with him, but out of respect for Cotton, I'd held back. As soon as I heard him call Ellie a whore, I was done. I charged forward and planted my balled fist into the side of his face, flaying his neck backward with a hard jolt. Before he had a chance to recover, I laid into him again and again. Neither Cotton, nor Stitch tried to stop me as I continued to beat the hell out of him. "If you ever disrespect her again, I'll fucking end you. Hell, I'd kill you right fucking now if I could."

With blood oozing from his nose and mouth, I reared back to hit him again. When he brought his hands up and tried to cover himself, I snarled, "Just look at you. You're nothing but a fucking pussy. Now you know how it feels. How Ellie felt every time you put your goddamn hands on her."

I kept wailing into him until I heard Cotton say, "Diesel."

I wanted nothing more than to keep going, but I held my hands up and I backed away. I looked over to Cotton and was about to apologize for losing my cool, but before I had a chance to speak, he gave me a chin lift, letting me off the hook. I stepped behind him and watched as he eased over to Brady. Cotton grabbed him by the collar, forcing him to look at him as he said, "Now, where were we?"

"I'm not making the call. Don't care what else you got to say."

"You know, it's only a matter of time before these guys step it up a notch, and you'll feel pain like you've never felt before."

"Maybe so, but I'll have the satisfaction of knowing that Ellie's rotting away in jail. That will get me through anything."

Stitch stepped forward, and with a calm, but eerie voice, he said, "Give me ten minutes."

"You got it," Cotton told him as he started for the door. I followed him out into the hall where Rip was still waiting for us.

"Having any luck?" Rip asked.

"Not yet, but we're giving Stitch a go at it." Cotton smirked.

He gave Cotton a disgruntled look. "Doubt he'll get him to budge. Hell, Tank's been working on him for days now, and he hasn't gotten anywhere with him."

"Don't take offense, but brother, *he's not Stitch*."

We stood by the door and waited to hear screams or pleads for mercy, *something*, but there was nothing, only silence. We all knew what Stitch was capable of doing. He was known for breaking the strongest of men, so while none of us had any idea what was going on in that room, I felt certain that he'd get the job done. Overcome with curiosity, I leaned towards the door, trying my best to hear anything, but again, only silence. We were still standing around and waiting when the door suddenly opened. With a blank expression, Stitch said, "Need a burner. He's ready."

Cotton reached into his back pocket and handed him the phone. Stitch took it, and then walked back over to Brady. "Make the call."

With his hands trembling, Brady took the phone from Stitch and started to dial the number. Stitch crossed his arms and glared at him with a fierceness that even made *me* feel uneasy. I had no idea what had transpired between the two of them, but when Brady started speaking, he said everything exactly the way it needed to be said. "Hey, Dad. Yeah, it's me." We could all hear his father's voice when he replied. It was clear that he was surprised, and it took Brady several attempts to calm him down. "I know you have lots of questions, but I need you to listen to me, Dad. It's important." He took a deep breath, then continued, "I fucked up. I fucked up bad, and I got myself into something that not even you can get me out of. I've had to leave town." Again, we heard his father's voice blaring through the other end of the phone. "Dad! Listen to me. I can't come back. I don't have a choice in it. This is the way it's gotta be, but I need you to do something for me."

His face twisted into a grimace as he forced himself to say, "I need you to help Ellie. You know I haven't done right by her. You know I've done pretty horrible stuff to her ... things she didn't deserve. Dad, you can't let her go to jail for something she didn't do. You gotta get the charges dropped. All of them." He grew silent as he listened to his father's response. "I don't care what you have to do. Just make it happen."

Stitch flicked his wrist, cueing him that his time was up and to end the call. "I need you to do this for me, Dad. *Please*." He sighed. "Thank you. I've got to go. Don't worry about me. I'm gonna be okay." He waited a moment before he said, "You, too, Dad."

The asshole was on the verge of tears as he hung up the phone and handed it to Stitch. We all watched as Stitch knelt down beside him. Brady's eyes grew wide with horror as Stitch whispered something to him. Suddenly, my respect for Stitch hit a whole new level, and I found myself smiling as I followed them out into the hall. Just as we were about to head back into the club-house, Cotton looked over to Rip and said, "I've got something in the SUV that you might be interested in."

"Really? What's that?"

"Just come see for yourself." Cotton led him over to the trunk, and once he opened it, he said, "I think this might belong to you."

"Well, fuck me rotten. Where did you find it?"

"Ellie had hidden it in the house. Wasn't sure it was yours until we got here," Cotton explained.

"Thanks, brother. Looks like we're officially done with Brady boy." Rip snickered.

"Can you hold on to him for a few more days ... just until we know that call worked in our favor?" Cotton requested.

"You got it, brother. Just give me a heads up when the coast is clear." Rip looked over to the gate and called out, "Hey, Dive. Come give me a hand with this."

Once they got everything unloaded, I went back inside to get Ellie. When I walked in, I found her sitting at the back table talking with the girl from behind the bar. As soon as I saw her, the tension I'd been carrying started to subside. I'd heard people talk about finding that person who made them see the world in a completely different way, and how they loved them like no other, but I never truly understood what they were talking about. For me, love was just a word—until Ellie came crashing into my life. I finally got it. With Ellie, I found something I didn't even know I was missing.

ELLIE

*a*s soon as he walked back into the bar, I knew something had happened. I could see it in his eyes. I wanted to go to him, ask him what it was, but I couldn't move. I was frozen in my seat—not because I was scared, but because I couldn't take my eyes off of him. I just sat there staring at him, the man I'd given my heart to, and I realized that I'd hadn't fallen for him because he was perfect, *because he wasn't*. Like everyone, he had his faults, those little imperfections that made him human, and he knew I had my own. He knew about my past and all my secrets, and instead of holding it against me, instead of treating me differently, he saw through them and found the real me beneath it all. Our imperfections were what made us work.

As he started towards me, Candi, one of their club's bartenders, leaned towards me and said, "Damn. He is *so* freaking hot."

She was practically drooling over him like he was a prize-winning bull at the market. "Yeah, he sure is."

I could hear the intrigue in her voice as she asked, "You two got something going, don't ya?"

"Yeah, you could say that."

"I thought so," she replied, trying to hide her disappointment. "I could tell he didn't want to leave you here alone, but I can't blame him for that. A looker like you is gonna draw some attention from the fellas. No doubt about that."

Candi was a beautiful girl, blonde-haired, blue-eyed, Barbie doll kind of beautiful, and it was hard not to feel flattered by her compliment. "I guess you could say he's the protective type."

"Smart man. Hold on to that one."

When Diesel finally made it over to us, he asked, "You ready to go?"

I nodded and hugged Candi goodbye before following him out into the parking lot. Once we were outside, I turned to him and asked, "What happened? Did you find out anything about Brady?"

He paused before he answered, "Can't tell you much, Ellie. Just that everything's gonna be okay."

"What do you mean *you can't tell me?*"

"I'll explain more later, but this all falls under club business ..." he started.

Before he could finish, Cotton came up behind him and interrupted, "Only gonna tell you this because I think it's important that you know. *You didn't kill Brady.*"

"How do you know that? Is he here?" When neither of them answered, I said, "If he's here, I want to see him."

Cotton's eyebrows furrowed as he growled, "That's not gonna happen, Ellie. Not a fucking chance."

"Please, Cotton. I need this. Just two minutes, so I can finally get some closure."

"You'll get all the closure you need when we get those charges dropped. Seeing him isn't gonna—"

Before he could finish, I said, "After all he's done to me, I just want a chance to look him in the eye and let him know that he didn't win. That's all I'm asking for here. Just a chance to—"

"Fine," Cotton grumbled. "You've got two minutes. That's it."

"That's all I'm asking for."

"I'll get Rip," Cotton told us as he turned and started back inside the clubhouse.

Once he was gone, Diesel put his hands on my shoulders and asked, "You sure about this?"

I nodded, but the nerves that were building in my stomach made me wonder if I was doing the right thing. "I think so."

"You don't have to do this."

I eased up on my tiptoes and kissed him. "*Yes*, I do. I hope you can understand that."

"I'm not sure that I do, but if this really means that much to you, I won't try to change your mind." He brought his hand up to my cheek. "But there's no way in hell I'm letting you do this alone."

I smiled as I said, "I didn't suspect you would."

It wasn't long before Cotton returned with the man he'd called Rip. Diesel and I followed them both to their garage, and the anxious feeling I had in the pit of my stomach only grew stronger as they led us through a back door and into an eerie hallway. When they reached a side door, Cotton turned back to me and said, "Before you go in, you should know ... he's in pretty rough shape."

I nodded and watched with great apprehension as he slowly opened the door. There were no windows and the lights were dim, and the foul smell burned my eyes, making it difficult to see as I walked into the room. But I didn't have to see clearly to know that Brady was in the room. I could feel it in my bones. I took another step forward and my stomach turned when I spotted him sitting on the bed. His eyes were bruised and swollen, but I could see the hatred in his glare. Cotton was right. He was in pretty rough shape, and if he was anyone else, I might've felt sorry for him. But I felt no pity, no remorse. When I looked at him, I felt nothing.

"Hello, Brady."

"What the hell do you want?"

Those familiar, anxious feelings started creeping over me, but I refused to let them stop me from what I needed to say. After inhaling a deep breath, I looked him in the eye as I said, "You know I didn't deserve those things you did to me, Brady. I was good to you, even when you gave me no reason to be."

"Don't come in here all high and mighty like you're some kind of goddamn saint. We both know the only reason you're here is because you've gotten yourself mixed up with these assholes." His face was red with fury as he spat, "I always knew you were a good-for-nothing whore, and now, you've just proven me right by getting tied up with those lowlife motherfuckers. Damn. A fucking biker club? Seriously?"

"I don't have to justify my actions to you, but I will tell

you this. Each and every one of those *bikers* are better men than you could ever be."

"I don't want to hear this shit, Ellie," he barked. "For fuck's sake. Just say what you gotta say and get the hell out of here."

"I'm leaving, but before I do, I want you to take one last look at me, Brady." I took a step closer to him as I said, "I want you to see that I'm still standing. After all you did, you didn't break me. You tried, but like everything else you ever tried to do, *you failed*. I don't know what's going to happen to you, but I do know this: My future looks a whole lot brighter than yours."

With that, I turned and looked over to Diesel. "I'm done here."

When we started out of the room, Diesel reached for my hand and gave it a gentle squeeze as we followed the others out of the garage. While we continued towards Cotton's SUV, I realized that I felt lighter, freer, than I had in years. I'd always believed that there were two types of forgiveness: the kind where you gave the person another chance, and the kind of forgiveness where you walked away. For Brady, there would be no more second chances. When I walked out of that room, I'd forgiven him for what he'd done to me, but I hadn't done it for him, I did it for myself. I was tired of carrying around the weight of resentment and anger and absolving him was the only way I'd ever be free from it.

Just as we were about to get in the truck, Diesel pulled me over to him and said, "You did good back there. I'm proud of you."

"I'm just glad it's over." I wrapped my arms around him and hugged him tightly. "Take me home."

It was several hours later before we finally made it back to Diesel's place. We hadn't eaten anything since breakfast, so Diesel fixed us a pot of spaghetti for dinner. Once we were finished eating, he made us a fire where we cuddled up on the sofa and watched TV in silence. It seemed both of us were lost in our own thoughts as we tried to come to terms with everything that had transpired at the Forsaken Saint's clubhouse. I was trying to figure out why I hadn't shared everything with him sooner. I wanted to think it was because I hadn't remembered, but the truth was, I had. By that time, I'd remembered everything. Maybe it was out of fear or simple embarrassment, but I'd kept it from him, and I didn't like that I did. Sensing that something was weighing on my mind, Diesel looked over to me and asked, "You okay?"

"Yes and no." I studied him for a moment, seeing the concern in his eyes, and in my heart, I felt like I could tell him anything. It was my mind that was having trouble understanding. "I'm sorry I didn't tell you about everything sooner. I'm not sure why I didn't."

"You've been through a lot, Ellie. There could be a number of reasons why. The fact is, you still told me."

"I think I was embarrassed."

"Embarrassed? Why would you be embarrassed?"

"Because I married a monster, and then I didn't even have the strength to get away from him. It took having something to blackmail him with before I found the courage—"

"Stop right there. You're being way too hard on yourself with all this. Instead of focusing on the things you didn't do, you need to focus on the things you did. *You got away.* That's all that matters."

"I think a part of me is worried that you might be too good to be true." The words slipped out before I had to think. "I mean—"

"I'm just me, Ellie. In time you'll see that. And in time, you'll also see that I'm not him. I'm nothing like him."

"I know you aren't him, Diesel. I've known that from the start."

"Then stop worrying about repeating your past, because you'll never enjoy what's ahead of you if you're always looking back." His voice was soft and heartfelt as he urged, "Be here with me. Let me show you how good things can really be."

"I'm here. There's no place I'd rather be."

As soon as the words left my mouth, Diesel leaned towards me. His intoxicating scent enveloped me, a mixture of cologne and fresh leather, seducing all my senses. Simply being this close to him made my heart start to race as it nearly leapt from my chest when he said, "You're amazing, Ellie, and I'm going to spend the rest of my life showing you just how amazing you really are."

His gorgeous, green eyes locked on mine as his mouth crashed down on my lips, kissing me with a fervent passion. My entire body tingled with desire as he delved into my mouth, and it was clear he was feeling the same when his fingers dug into the sides of my waist, pulling me closer to him. The bristles of his day-old beard lightly scratched against my skin as he took complete control, making my body ache for more while he claimed me with his mouth. A light moan escaped from my throat as my hands began to roam over his chest, gliding over the bulging muscles of his abdomen. I wanted to touch his bare skin, feel his body pressed against mine, and I couldn't wait a moment longer. I reached for his shirt, and he pulled it off his body. Once it was gone, our hands became frantic, quickly removing the remaining clothes that separated us. In just a few seconds, I was wearing only my lace bra and panties.

"You're every fantasy I've ever had," I whispered as my eyes roamed over his body, traveling along the lines and curves of the muscles in his chest, then looking back to his gorgeous face as I smiled in appreciation. His eyes were focused on my nearly naked body, and my heart skipped a beat when I noticed the desire in his appraisal. I watched with fascination as his chest slowly rose and fell with each tortured breath.

"Mine," slipped through his lips just before he reached for me, pulling me in for another heated kiss. His hands slowly eased behind my back to release the clasp of my bra. As the fabric slipped away from my body, I felt his lips glide across my skin to my breast. "Every inch of you is mine, and I'm going to cherish you in ways you've never imagined."

The glow of the fire danced in his eyes as he lowered me down on the sofa. He hovered over me for a brief moment, and then his mouth resumed its divine torture of kissing and nipping the delicate skin of my neck. He settled in between my thighs, and I lifted my hips towards him as I tried desperately to find relief for the burning need that was building up inside me.

"Yes," I hissed as his hand slowly slid between our bodies. He traced his fingers across my panties, teasing me with his light caresses before pushing the fabric to the side. He casually slid his fingers inside me, tormenting me as he swirled them ever so slowly. I could feel the fiery hunger and yearning deep inside me. It had started with just a spark, but I could feel it building, my arousal smoldering as it spread through my body. That feeling only intensified when his thumb began circling my swollen clit, drawing out my pleasure. When he found my G-spot, my breath caught in my lungs, and as my orgasm took hold, the muscles in my body started quivering uncontrollably. I was still trying to catch my breath when I felt my panties being slipped down over my hips.

I turned to look at him standing before me and watched anxiously as he tore the condom wrapper with his teeth. After he slowly slid it down his long, hard shaft, he lowered himself down on top of me. His weight pressed me into the cushions, making my entire body tremble with anticipation. This man had me spellbound, and I found myself gazing at him, then feverishly touching him, just to be sure he wasn't a dream. A needful moan pulsed through his chest as his hands, rough and impatient, roamed over my entire body, proof that this was no dream. He was real, all of him, and my body melted into his as he trailed delicate kisses over my breasts, scraping his teeth across my sensitive flesh. He hovered over me, and a warmth spread across my flesh as I watched his eyes wander over every inch of my bare skin.

"You're so beautiful, Ellie," he whispered with his breath caressing my neck. Emotion flashed through his eyes as he settled between my legs, and then he stopped and inhaled a long, strained breath. Seeing that he was trying to maintain his control, I placed my palms on his chest and whispered, "Don't hold back, Scotty. Not with me."

He clenched his jaw before lifting my hips and making one forceful thrust deep inside me, filling me completely. My fingers tangled in his hair, as I wrapped my legs around him, taking him deeper inside me. Being with him was different than anything I'd ever experienced. He made me feel whole, undamaged, and beautiful; the feeling was bliss. Pure bliss.

I wanted to slowly savor the moment, to feel every erotic sensation, but he had other plans. He growled as his pace quickened, becoming more demanding and intense with each shift of his hips. My hands curled around his back as I held onto him, bracing myself for the next wave of pleasure that teetered on crashing through my body. His eyes never left mine as he increased his rhythm, each thrust more forceful than the last. My inner muscles clenched around him as I felt another orgasm building inside me. "Oh, God! Don't stop!" I pleaded.

I could feel my climax burning through my veins. His very touch sent me spiraling out of control—body and soul—and the feeling was so exhilarating that I was finding it difficult to even breathe. I couldn't stop my greedy body from seeking its ultimate high, and with one last, deep thrust, the fire raged inside me, consuming me as I reached the apex of euphoric pleasure. I let out a strangled cry as I writhed beneath him. Even with my body shuddering from the aftermath of such intense carnal satisfaction, he didn't slow. Not even close. He drove into me again and again until he found his own release—with the growl of a bear whose hunger had been sated—as he lowered his body on top of mine. I lay there limp beneath him as I listened to the rapid beating of his heart. It slowly began to return to a steady pace, and then, he eased off of me. As he started walking towards the bathroom, my eyes dropped to his incredibly sexy behind. Like he could read my mind, he looked over his shoulder with a cocky smirk and asked, "Are you enjoying the view?"

"Yes. Very much." I giggled. "Walk slower, will ya!"

Shaking his head, he chuckled. "I've created a monster."

"Are you saying that's a bad thing?"

"Absolutely not. I wouldn't have it any other way."

DIESEL

here was nothing worse than waiting, especially when my future with Ellie was hanging in the balance. I'd called Cotton more times than I could count, hoping that he'd heard something from MJ, but there was no news. The charges against Ellie were still in full effect, and the prosecution was continuing its investigation. Big had been using his hacking skills to keep tabs on anything that they might uncover, and as far as he could tell, they'd found nothing. MJ assured us that even if the chief didn't do as Brady had asked, the lack of evidence would make it nearly impossible for them to prove that Ellie had actually done anything wrong. Even so, I prayed that we'd never have to find out. I wanted the charges dropped and for her to be free and clear of Brady for good.

While neither of us had said it out loud, Ellie and I were both feeling pretty anxious, and just sitting at the house wasn't helping any. Hoping if we kept ourselves distracted, we might ease some of the tension, I suggested, "You up for getting out for a little while?"

"Sure. Where do you want to go?"

"I thought I might take you out to Smokey's place."

"What's at Smokey's?"

"His folks had an apple orchard when he was growing up, and after they died, they left the place to him and his sister. They've built it up to a really cool place, especially the barn. I thought we might go check it out."

"So, this doesn't have anything to do with MJ?" she asked with a knowing smile.

I shrugged. "Well, if we happen to see her, it wouldn't hurt to ask if she's heard anything."

"Okay, but I'm pretty sure you're driving everybody crazy at this point. You've already called Cotton like ten times since we left," she teased.

"I've only called him three times, thank you very much. I can't help it if I'm a little on edge. This is my girl we're talking about. I need to know everything's gonna be okay."

"Your girl, huh?"

"Yeah. My girl. Now, quit giving me a hard time." I put my hands on her hips, pulling her towards me, and after a quick kiss, I said, "Grab your coat."

When we got outside, I noticed that it had finally gotten warm enough to clear off the roads. It wouldn't be long until the tow company had gotten Ellie's car pulled from the ravine. Since it was totaled, we'd have to find her something else to drive, but that was a task for another day. We both needed some time to decompress, and as I started towards the truck, I found myself wishing it was warm enough for us to take the bike. Ellie must've noticed my hesitation and asked, "Do you want to take your bike?"

"I'm afraid it will be too cold for you. It gets pretty chilly when you're going down the road at sixty to seventy miles per hour."

"Well, I thought a biker was always prepared for whatever kind of weather came their way," she mocked.

"We are."

"Alright then." Her voice was full of sass when she asked, "Don't you have some more warm stuff I could put on?"

"Yeah." I nodded with a smile. "I've got some heated gear you could use."

"Great. I'm up for taking the bike if you are."

"I'm definitely up for it," I told her, trying not to sound overly excited. "Let me go get my gear."

I went into the garage and grabbed my heated jacket and pants for her and an extra layer of thermal wear for myself. Once we were both dressed, I gave her a hand with the helmet, hopped on my Harley, and helped her climb on. "Have you ever ridden before?"

"Just my brother's moped."

"Not quite the same thing, angel."

"Okay. Then, what do I need to know?"

"Just hold on tight, lean into the turns, and try not to wiggle when we're coming up to a stop. Follow my lead with the rest, and you'll be fine."

"Got it."

With Ellie clinging to my sides, I slowly backed out of the driveway and out onto the main road. It had been weeks since I'd been able to ride, and just feeling the engine roar to life gave me a rush. It wasn't hard to describe the intense feelings of riding a motorcycle. It was the best high I've ever had. There was something about the wind in my face, even when it was freezing-ass cold outside, that made me feel alive. All of my senses were magnified—I became one with the road and the world around me, with all its different smells and breathtaking colors. It was simply incredible. Absolutely nothing beat the thrill of riding a six hundred pound, two-wheeled machine, and knowing the risks involved, only heightened my enjoyment. It was the best therapy known to man, at least for me it was.

As we drove down the old, country road to Smokey's house, I was worried that Ellie might not be feeling the same way, but then she leaned forward, her lips close to my ear, and shouted, "This is amazing!"

"Glad you think so. Are you warm enough?"

"I'm freezing! But I love it!"

I didn't like the fact that she was cold, but I hoped she'd be able to warm up once we got to Smokey's. When we pulled up their driveway, there were several cars parked in front of the barn. Even though it was off-season, people still came to buy Liv's canned goods, along with other little odds and ends. As soon as we were parked, I helped her off the bike and out of her gear, and we entered the barn. They were still remodeling, but the place already looked amazing. I couldn't believe how much MJ had gotten done, especially since she was still working part-time at the law office. Seeing how well they were doing, I figured it was only a matter of time before she'd be working at the farm full-time.

Smokey was in the back, talking with one of his field hands, and as soon as Ellie spotted him, she looked over to me and whispered, "Is it just me, or does Smokey remind you of a mountain man?"

"A mountain man?" I chuckled.

"Yeah. With his dark eyes and big, bushy, black beard, he reminds me of a mountain man ... especially with that flannel shirt he's wearing."

"Never thought of it before, but now that you mention it, I guess he does." As we started walking towards him, I said, "How's it going, Smoke?"

"Hey." He smiled. "I didn't know you were coming out today."

"We were getting a little stir crazy at the house and decided to get out for a bit. Ellie hasn't had a chance to see the place, so I thought we'd stop by."

"Glad you came by, but MJ isn't here. She had a doctor's appointment, and then she was gonna run over to her office for something, but it shouldn't be much longer."

I nodded. "Mind if I show Ellie around for a bit?"

"No, not at all. Why don't you take one of the UTVs and go for a spin around the orchard? There are a couple of blankets in the back of mine that you're welcome to use."

"We'll do that. Thanks, brother."

We headed outside and over to Smokey's big, red UTV, and, like he said, there were several blankets in the back-seat. I handed one to Ellie, and once she'd covered her legs, I started driving out towards the orchard. Even though they weren't blooming, the fields of trees were beautiful. One row led into the next, making the farm seem even larger than it really was. We hadn't been riding long, when Ellie said, "I've never been to an apple orchard before."

"Well, what do you think?"

"It's beautiful. If I was Smokey, I don't think I would ever leave."

"Believe it or not, he'd told me that he wasn't exactly thrilled about taking the place over."

"Really? Why not?"

"Too many memories and too much work, although, he's got good people working for him. That always makes it easier," I explained.

"I'm sure it does. I imagine it's a lot of hard work, but I think I'd love it."

"Well, I know the boss." I gave her a quick wink. "If you ever decide you want to work out here, I could put a good word in for you."

"I don't know what I'll do. I've always wanted to take a few classes, but I think that time has come and gone."

"What kind of classes?"

"Just some art classes. Maybe, using watercolors or even graphic design. There was a time when I was pretty good at it. My high school teacher said I had a lot of promise, but that was years ago."

"Why'd you stop?"

"I don't know. I guess I lost my inspiration." She turned and looked back out at the orchard. "But I think I've found it again."

"Then, we'll find you some classes to take," I told her as I started driving back towards the barn.

"You make it sound so simple."

"It is simple. If there's something you want to do, I'll do whatever it takes to make it happen. Easy as that."

Tears started to fill her eyes as she said, "Diesel."

"What's with the waterworks? Did I say something wrong?"

"No. You said everything just right. You always do." She leaned her head on my shoulder as she whispered, "I don't know if my heart can take much more."

"Meant every word, Ellie. You're mine, and I take care of what's mine." I felt her tremble and worried that the cold was getting to her. I reached behind us for another blanket, and as I handed it to her, I said, "I better get you back before you turn into a popsicle."

When we got back to the barn, there was still no sign of MJ, but Smokey was done working and asked us inside for a cup of coffee. I figured it would give Ellie a chance to warm up before the ride home, so I took him up on his offer. Ellie's eyes grew wide as we stepped into his house. I couldn't blame her. It was really something. The house came with the farm, and as soon as he took it over, Smokey had Guardrail and the guys completely remodel the entire house. Every room looked like something out of a magazine, but even with all the fancy touches, it still felt welcoming, like a home should be. Once Smokey poured us each some coffee, he said, "I heard you two had a pretty interesting visit with the Saints."

"Yeah. You could say that."

"Maybe it'll all pay off soon, especially since the chief knows his son is still alive."

I shrugged. "You'd think that, but we haven't heard anything from the prosecutor. Gotta make you wonder what's taking so long."

"If it was my guess, I'd say he's out there looking for

him, but we both know he's not gonna find him. Maybe, it's just a matter of getting it out of his system."

"Maybe so, but I gotta tell ya, this waiting is for the fucking birds, brother." I looked over to Ellie and sighed. "We're both ready to get this thing done."

Ellie looked over to Smokey and said, "It's just hard to think about making plans for my future until all this gets settled. I guess I should've thought about all this before I turned myself in, huh?"

"We all get why you did it, Ellie," Smokey told her. "Took a lot of balls to face up to that, and I got no doubt that it'll all work out in your favor, especially with MJ and the brothers having your back. You'll see."

"You've all been so good to me. I don't know what I would've done without you."

"Glad you don't have to find out." Smokey smiled. "How are you liking it out at Diesel's place?"

"I love it there, and the views are incredible."

"Yeah, they are. He really lucked out the day he found it."

We were just finishing up our cup of coffee, when we heard a car pull up in the driveway. Smokey tilted his head and as he looked out the window, his eyes lit up. "There she is."

As badly as I wanted to rush out that door to talk to her, I stayed planted in my seat and waited for her to come inside. When she finally walked in, it was clear from the way she tossed her bags on the table that she'd had a long day.

"Hey, guys. Smokey didn't tell me you were coming by."

"They haven't been here long. Diesel brought Ellie

over to see the orchard. How did the doctor's appointment go?"

She ran her hand over her full belly as she smiled. "Good. The doctor says she's doing great."

"I told you." Smokey boasted.

"Yes, you did, but you know I'm gonna worry. It's what I do." MJ walked over to Ellie and said, "I have some things to talk to you about."

"Okay."

MJ took a step back and cocked her head to the side. "So, what do you want first, the good news or the bad news?"

The moment had finally arrived. Even though it hadn't been all that long, it seemed like we'd been waiting a lifetime to find out if Ellie's charges were going to be dropped. Not knowing what she was about to say, I tried to mentally prepare myself for the worst. Apparently, Ellie was doing the same, because she said, "Give me the bad news first."

ELLIE

*M*y mind was racing as I waited for MJ to drop the bomb. I could tell from the expression on her face that she was worried, and fearing that I wasn't going to like what she had to say, I suddenly had the urge to dart out of the room. I'd had enough bad news, and I wasn't sure I could handle any more. Just as my anxiety hit an all-time high, Diesel reached for my hand, taking it in his as he stood next to me. I took a deep breath as MJ said, "I just heard from Brady's father."

Diesel didn't sound all that surprised when he replied, "Oh, really?"

"Yes. He wants to talk," MJ continued.

"To who?" I asked.

"You. He'd like to meet with you tomorrow morning."

"So, that's the bad news?" I asked. "Why is that bad? It's not like I *have to* meet with him."

MJ grimaced. "Well … That's just it. Your good news is tied into the bad."

"How so?"

"He said that he had information that would help your case, but he won't share unless you agree to meet with him."

"Damn," Smokey grumbled. "Gotta wonder what that's all about."

"Maybe he thinks I know something about Brady."

"I don't care what he thinks." Diesel turned to MJ and growled, "You can tell him to fuck off. There's no way in hell that she's gonna have a meet with that piece of shit."

"*Diesel.*" I tried my best to keep my voice from wavering as I said, "I can do this. I may not like it, but I can do it."

"I know you can, Ellie, but that's not the point. There's no reason for you to be subjected to his bullshit. Not after everything they did to you."

"Whether we like it or not, if he can help with the case, I have to go."

MJ stepped forward and said, "She won't be there alone, Diesel. I'll be there, and for that matter, you and Cotton can go, too. We'll meet at the coffee shop and let them talk. If anything goes wrong, we'll be there."

Diesel's expression softened, but I could tell he still wasn't convinced. "I can handle Brady's father, Diesel. He's not like his son. I know he didn't always do the right thing, especially where I was concerned, but he had good intentions. He loved his son and just wanted to help him the best he could. There was no way for him to know that he was just making a bigger mess of things."

Before Diesel had a chance to respond, Smokey turned to him and said, "You're gonna need to talk to Cotton before either of you make a decision on this, 'cause in the end, the final call is up to him."

MJ gave him a slight smile as she shrugged. "I called him as soon as I got the call from the chief."

"And?" Diesel pushed.

"Like you, he wasn't exactly thrilled," MJ started. "But he seems to think that we have to go along with his request if we want to get Ellie's charges dropped."

"And we can both be there?"

"In the coffee shop is fine, but he wants to speak with her alone."

"Fine. Set it up," Diesel ordered. "But if there's any bullshit whatsoever, I'm taking her out of there."

"Understood." MJ then turned her attention to me. "We need to talk about what you're going to say tomorrow."

"Okay."

"If he brings up the shooting, try to be as vague as possible. Don't give him any specifics. If you can, try to steer away from that topic altogether."

"Okay."

"I know you can do this. This isn't an official interrogation, but we still need to be careful. You don't want to tell him something that he can use against you."

"I got it."

She smiled. "Good. Now, try not to worry about it too much. We'll be right there with you the whole time."

"Thanks, MJ."

After we said our goodbyes, we walked out to the bike. With the sun starting to fall, the ride home was a bit colder, but it was worth it to see the effect it had on Diesel. By the time we arrived back at the house, he seemed to be a little less tense, but I could tell that he was still worried. He was quiet and withdrawn, and as soon as we'd finished dinner, he said, "I need to run over to the clubhouse."

"Why? Is something wrong?"

"No. I just need to talk to Cotton about something. Nothing for you to worry about."

"Okay."

"Do you want to come along?"

I hoped that talking to him might improve his mood, so I decided to let him go alone. "If it's okay with you, I'll just stay here and take a hot bath."

"You sure?"

"Yes." I leaned forward and kissed him on his cheek. "I'm sure. Just don't take too long."

"I won't," he assured me.

After my bath, I crawled into bed, and I was just starting to doze off when Diesel came walking through the door. Without saying a word, he crawled in next to me and wrapped his arm around my waist. He lowered his mouth to my ear, and I could feel the heat of his breath as he whispered, "Hey."

I rolled over to face him. "Hey there, handsome. Is everything okay?"

He pulled me over to him, and I laid my head down on his chest. "It is now."

"I know you're worried about tomorrow, but everything is going to be okay."

"I'm the one who's supposed to be saying that to you." He chuckled. "But you're right. Everything's gonna be fine. I'm gonna make sure of it."

"I know you will."

He kissed me softly on the top of my head and said,

"Get some sleep, angel. Something tells me that tomorrow is going to be a long one."

I closed my eyes and tried to fall asleep, but every time I drifted off, I'd wake back up shortly after. The vicious cycle of dozing in and out of sleep started to wear on me, and after several hours, I finally gave up. Trying to be as quiet as I could, I eased out of bed and went to the living room, where I spent the rest of the night watching some silly horror flick on TV. By the time Diesel finally woke up, it was time for us to get ready to go, so I finished my cup of coffee and went to take a shower. When I came out, Diesel was waiting for me in the living room. "You ready?"

"Almost." I walked over to him and wrapped my arms around his waist, hugging him tightly. I inhaled a deep breath, taking in his scent and warmth, and after a brief moment I let him go. I looked up at him and said, "Okay. Now, I'm ready."

"You sure you want to do this?"

"We both know I don't have a choice. Let's just get this thing over with once and for all."

I followed him out to the truck, and once I was settled inside, we headed towards the coffee shop. When we arrived, MJ and Cotton were already there. Tensions were running high as we each took a moment to greet one another and were only made worse when the chief's car pulled up in front of the shop. My back stiffened as I watched him open his car door, and I was trying to mentally prepare myself for what waited ahead when Cotton called out to me. "Ellie?"

"Yes?"

"Remember what MJ told you. Keep it simple, and if

he asks you where Brady is, you have to make him believe that you know nothing, that you haven't seen him since the night you left the house."

I nodded. "I've got it."

I walked over to one of the empty tables up front and sat down. My heart was pounding as I waited for him to come inside, and when he finally walked through the door, I thought it would beat right out of my chest. Once he saw me, he gave me a small smile and said, "Hello, Ellie."

"Hi, Grayson. It's good to see you."

"Not sure that you mean that, but it's nice of you to say." He pulled out his chair and as he sat down, he took a quick glance around the room. A flicker of animosity flashed through his eyes when he spotted Cotton and Diesel sitting with MJ. "I see you brought your friends along."

"I did," I answered dryly.

"Not sure I know what to think about that. Do you have any idea who those people really are?"

"I know enough."

"They're criminals, Ellie. They make a living by selling drugs and guns all over—"

Before he could continue, I stopped him by saying, "Maybe so, but these so called criminals treat me better than your son ever did and he was an officer of the law! Besides, I'm sure you didn't ask to meet with me just so you could tell me about the men of Satan's Fury."

"No. I guess I didn't."

"Good. So, why don't you tell me what this is really all about? Why did you want to see me?"

Just as he was about to answer, one of the waitresses came over to the table. "Can I get you two something?"

"I'll have a cup of coffee. Black. Two creams and one sugar. How about you, Ellie?"

"I'll have a small mocha, thank you."

When she walked away, Chief Blackwell turned his attention back to me. He studied me a moment before he said, "You've always been such a beautiful girl. I can see why my son was so crazy about you."

Annoyed by his comment, I grumbled, "Yeah ... crazy is a good word for it."

"I remember the day he came home and told me the two of you were getting married. I have to admit that I wasn't exactly thrilled about it. I thought you were too young, but he was adamant about doing right by you."

"And when he beat me to the point that I lost your granddaughter, was he doing right by me then?" I snapped.

"What are you talking about?" His voice trembled. "Brady said you were in a car accident."

"What about the time I shattered my collarbone, or the time I broke my wrist? Did he tell you that those were accidents, too?"

"There must be some misunderstanding—"

Unable to contain my anger, I interrupted him again. "And what about all the police reports that were never filed? Were they just misunderstandings, or did you know exactly what you were doing when you got rid of them?"

He didn't respond. He simply sat there staring at me, and I could see the torment in his eyes as he thought about everything I'd said. Brady had been feeding him nothing but lies for years, and I had no doubt that it was difficult for him to hear what had really happened. He remained silent until his face twisted in anger and he growled, "Is that why you turned against him? Because you blamed *him* for losing the baby?"

For a brief moment, I actually thought he was starting to accept the terrible truth about his son, but he wasn't. He couldn't accept the truth because it was simply easier to believe otherwise. Unfortunately for him, I was done living with the lies. "Did you know that I actually had to deliver the baby that night? I held your granddaughter in my arms, and she was the most beautiful thing I'd ever seen."

"Answer my question!"

I tried to keep my voice from quivering as I said, "She still felt warm to the touch. I almost couldn't believe that she was really dead. Brady felt awful about what he'd done, and for a long time after that, he tried to make things right between us. But there was something broken inside of him, and no matter how hard I tried, I couldn't fix it. And neither could you."

He leaned forward, placing his elbows on the table as he stared at me with pleading eyes. "Just tell me where he is. Let me try to help him, please."

For a split second, I actually felt compassion for the man. Like any loving parent, he still had hope for his son, unfortunately, I knew differently. There was nothing in this world that could change a man like Brady, so I told him, "I don't know where he is, Grayson, and quite frankly, I don't want to know. As far as I'm concerned, he can stay gone."

"You honestly expect me to believe that you don't have any idea where he could be?"

"Yes. Why shouldn't you believe me? Brady never told me anything. He never told me how he could afford his new car or how he managed to buy that new house. I knew better than to ask him, because I knew there would be hell to pay if I did. So, I just left it alone and tried to make the best of a bad situation."

"Brady was a good boy."

"Maybe, at one point he was a *good boy*, but he wasn't a good man. You and I both know that. I finally let go of the hope that he could ever be better, and maybe it's time that you do the same."

"I can't give up on my son. He's all I've got."

"That's not exactly true. You have your wife and your career. You've worked hard to get where you are, and you need to hold on to that."

"And Brady?" he asked with dread.

"If what the news is saying is true, he's gone, and he obviously doesn't want to be found. We both know if that changes, you'll be the first one he turns to."

I wanted to ask him about the evidence he had about my case, but I decided to leave it alone. I would just have to hope that he would keep his word and share what he had with the prosecutor. Having nothing else to say, I stood up and started to walk back towards Diesel. I'd only taken a few steps when I heard him say, "I'm sorry, Ellie. For all those things he did to you."

His words caught me by surprise, and tears stung my eyes as I turned back to him and said, "Thank you for saying that, Grayson. I really do hope that you can find some peace in all this. I wish there was more that I could do to help."

"If you hear anything ..."

"I'll call you." I lied. "Take care of yourself."

By the time I made it back to Diesel, I was relieved to see that he was already gone. As soon as I sat down, MJ asked, "How did it go?"

"Better than I expected."

"Did he ask about Brady?"

"Yes, but I didn't tell him anything. I basically told him it was time to let him go. I'm not sure if he listened, but I guess we will see." I shrugged. "I'm just glad that's over. I could use a drink, a hot bath, and a nap."

"I'm just the guy who can make that happen," Diesel replied with a smile. He stood up, and we all followed him out into the parking lot. Before we went out to the truck, Diesel turned to Cotton and asked, "Did you get that thing taken care of?"

Cotton nodded. "Just let me know when, and you can consider it handled."

"Thanks, brother."

As soon as we got back in Diesel's truck, I asked, "What was that about?"

"Something." He smirked.

"So, you're not going to tell me?"

"Nope."

"Seriously?" I pushed.

"You'll see soon enough."

DIESEL

꧁꧂

*W*hen I got home from the coffee shop, Ellie
told me everything that was said between
her and the chief. I respected the fact that he was the kind
of man who wanted to stand by his family, his son, but I
hoped that he would finally see the man his son truly was.
Brady deserved whatever he got for hurting Ellie. She'd
been through so much, but she'd come out on the other
side. I was proud of her for standing up for herself, yet
again, and I hoped her words would be the final push to
get the chief to do what he needed to make this right for
Ellie. Thankfully, two agonizing days later, we got the call
from MJ. She informed us that the charges against Ellie
had been reduced. While we were relieved, we still had no
idea what they were reduced to, and we wouldn't know
until they met with the prosecutor.

Ellie was a nervous wreck on the way to the prosecutor's. I tried to convince her that everything was going to
be okay, but she wasn't buying it. She and I both had
hoped that the charges would've been dropped

completely, but since she confessed with explicit details, there was no way she could walk away without some kind of repercussion. MJ was waiting for us when we walked into his office. "He's waiting for us in the conference room."

"Okay," Ellie replied anxiously.

"I'll be waiting right here for you when you come out," I assured her.

Ellie turn to MJ and asked, "Can Diesel come with us?"

"Yeah, I think that'll be okay." Before she started to walk down the hallway, MJ looked at me and said, "Leave the talking to me."

"You got it, boss."

When we walked into the conference room, John Pruitt, the prosecutor, stood up and adjusted his suit jacket and motioned us inside. "Come on in and have a seat."

The room reminded me of an upscale version of our meeting room at the clubhouse. It was small with a long, rectangular table and leather chairs surrounding it, and there were large, abstract watercolors lining the walls. As she sat down, MJ smiled and said, "Thanks for meeting with us today, John. I know your schedule is crazy busy."

"It is, but I managed to move a few things around." He spoke to MJ like we weren't sitting there as he said, "I'd like to get this case resolved today so we can put this all behind us."

"Sounds good to me." She reached into her briefcase and pulled out Ellie's file. "You mentioned on the phone that the charges against Ms. Blackwell have been reduced."

"They have. I've written up a plea bargain." Still

speaking like we weren't in the room, he casually slid the paper over to her. "If your client agrees to sign, we can call it a day."

Ellie leaned over to MJ as she asked, "What is a plea bargain?"

"It's an agreement between you and the prosecutor where you plead guilty to a specific charge in return for some concession from the prosecutor."

"In English?"

Before she could respond, the prosecutor looked at Ellie with disapproval and answered, "If you plead guilty to providing false information to law enforcement concerning your husband's missing person's case, we won't press for jail time. This particular offense can carry misdemeanor or even felony penalties, but the fact that you have no prior convictions, and considering your state of mind at the time of your confession, we've decided that counseling would benefit you the most."

"Counseling?"

"Yes. Six to eight months of weekly sessions with a therapist of your choosing. If you agree, then we can consider this case closed."

I couldn't believe it. The deal seemed too good to be true. It was everything we'd hoped for, and I thought we had it in the bag until I heard Ellie mumble, "But, I—"

MJ quickly lifted her hand and placed it on Ellie's arm, signaling her to stop talking. "I need a moment with my client."

He nodded, and then I heard her say, "He's throwing you a bone, Ellie. You won't get another one, I assure you. This may not seem perfect, but you need to sign those papers."

"Okay."

MJ turned her attention back to Mr. Pruitt and inquired, "And the counseling can be done at any location the client chooses?"

"Yes. I will just need the name and address of the counselor, so I can add it to the summary."

"Great. She'll agree to the deal."

"I was hoping you'd say that."

It seemed like we'd been riding on a fucking roller-coaster for days, but thankfully, the ride was finally coming to a stop. MJ eased the papers over to Ellie, and after handing her a pen, she showed her exactly where she needed to sign. Once she was done, MJ handed them over to Mr. Pruitt. "I guess that just about does it."

He extended his hand and said, "It was a pleasure working with you, MJ. I look forward to the next time."

"Thank you, John. I appreciate your help with all this."

Once we were done, MJ followed us back out to my truck and said to Ellie, "I'll ask around and see if I can get some info on any highly-recommended counselors in the area. Once you've made your decision, I'll send everything to John, so he can add it to your file."

"Okay. That sounds good."

"Oh, and I forgot to tell you. The judge signed your divorce papers. I know it's just a technicality, but it's official. You're divorced."

Ellie gave her a slight shrug. "As crazy as this may sound, it really doesn't change anything. Our marriage ended before it ever started, so you're right ... it was just a technicality, but thank you for handling that for me."

"No problem, sweetie." She winked and added, "Now, you two don't have too much fun celebrating tonight."

"We'll try, but I'm not making any promises." I teased. "You and that bun in the oven be careful going back home." Then Ellie paused for a second before turning in her direction and called out, "MJ! Thank you so very much. For everything." She simply gave us a warm smile and waved.

Once she was gone, I looked down at my watch to check the time. I had a surprise planned for Ellie when we got back to the house, and even though it was a three-hour drive back home, I was afraid they still might not be done. Hoping to kill some time, I suggested, "You wanna grab a bite to eat before we head back?"

"Sure, that sounds great."

Remembering the diner where Cotton and I had eaten, I took her hand and led her across the street. We each ordered a burger and fries, and as we started eating, Ellie said, "I can't believe it's really over, can you?"

"I gotta admit. I didn't think it would be that easy."

"It makes me wonder what the chief told them."

"Doesn't really matter now, but I'm glad he did the right thing."

A hopeful look crossed Ellie's face as she asked, "Can I ask a favor?"

"You know you can. What's on your mind?"

"Since we're in town, do you mind if we run by to see my parents? We don't have to stay long. I just wanted to tell them the good news, and let Dad know he'll be getting his bail money back soon."

"Absolutely, and we can stay as long as you like."

Once we were back in the truck, Ellie gave me the directions to her parents' place, and after a twenty-minute drive, we pulled up to their house. It was a small, white ranch-style home with a good bit of fenced-in land behind it, and from the similarities of another fence surrounding the fields, it looked like they owned that as well. We'd barely parked when a woman stepped out of the front door, and the minute I saw her dark hair and penetrating, dark eyes, I knew she was Ellie's mother. Ellie opened the door and rushed over to her, and in a blink of an eye, they were both crying as they hugged one another. As I started towards them, I heard Ellie say, "I'm so sorry, Mom. I'm so, so sorry."

"No, sweet girl. It's me who's sorry. I should've done so many things differently," her mother cried.

When she noticed that I had come up behind them, Ellie turned to her mother and said, "I'd like you to meet Scotty."

"It's very nice to meet you, Scotty. I'm Eleanor." She motioned for us to follow as she said, "It's freezing out here. Let's go inside and get you two warmed up."

Just as we were stepping inside, I heard Ellie's father say, "I told you she'd come."

"Hi, Dad." Ellie smiled as she glanced around the living room. "It still looks the same."

"There are some things that are different," Eleanor announced. "Your father bought the Turner's land a few years back. He's expanded the farm to almost four hundred acres."

"That's really great, Dad. I'm really proud for both of you." As soon as the words left her mouth, her expression changed. Her eyes narrowed with concern as she asked, "Wait. Is that how you got my bail money?"

"Yes, dear. He used it as collateral," Eleanor explained. "But don't you worry about that. We'd do it again to help."

Hoping to ease the tension that was building in the room, I stepped forward and said, "Why don't you tell them your good news?"

"You'll be getting your money back soon. My case was closed this morning."

"With everything that has taken place, we may not have the right to ask, but please, will you tell us *what* happened?" her father asked.

"I'll tell you all of it, but you should probably sit first. It's not going to be an easy story to hear," Ellie explained.

Once we were all seated, Ellie told them everything that had transpired over the past eight years, including how she'd lost the baby. As she spoke, her parents wept, and I could see the heartache and guilt on their faces as they heard the horrific things that had happened to their daughter. I couldn't imagine how they must've felt, but it was hard to feel sorry for them. The choices they made had a lasting effect on them all, and things could've been different if they'd just accepted that their daughter was strong-willed, but still, in fact, their daughter. I just hoped that they'd all learned from their past mistakes and could move forward, mending what was broken between them. Once she'd finished telling them everything, Eleanor went over to Ellie and hugged her as she cried, "I just don't understand. Why wouldn't you answer our calls or letters? We could've—"

"What letters?" Ellie interrupted.

"We wrote you all the time, Ellie. And we tried calling, but it always went to your voicemail. I thought you were just avoiding us."

"I never received any letters, Mom. And I certainly

never got any phone calls. I thought the both of you were still angry with me for leaving."

And just like that, Brady proved once again just how much of a lowlife, piece of shit he was. Enraged, I turned to Ellie and said, "I'm guessing Brady didn't want you talking to your folks. He probably blocked their number from your phone and intercepted all the letters before you had a chance to see them."

"I can't believe he did that." My heart ached for her as I watched tears stream down her face. "He knew how hurt I was."

"Honey, there's no way any of us could know what that boy was thinking. We've just got to focus on the future and try to put the past behind us."

"Your mother's right. I'm just glad you finally got free of him." Her father turned his attention to me and said, "I want to thank you for helping my daughter like you did. I owe you a great deal."

"It wasn't just me. She had the whole club looking out for her," I explained.

"Not sure I really understand all the club talk, but I will forever be indebted to you all for what you've done."

"I'll explain more about the club later," Ellie told him. "Maybe during my next visit."

"I'd like that. I'd like that a lot, and bring your friend when you come," he replied.

"I will." She glanced around the room as she asked, "What about Joseph? What is he doing these days?"

"Your brother is overseas," Eleanor told her with a pained expression. "He joined the army a few months after you left. He's been home a couple of times, but not for long. I think it was just too hard for him to be here without you. Maybe that will change now."

"Can you give me his number or email? I'd really like to reach out to him, if that's okay?"

"Of course." Her mother jotted the information down on a piece of paper, then handed it to her. "He would love to hear from you."

"Thanks." She looked down at her watch and stood up. "It's getting late, and we have a long drive back. I guess we better get going."

I said a quick goodbye to each of them and stepped outside to give Ellie a moment alone with her folks. A few minutes later, she came outside with a smile. "Thank you so much for this. It was really good to see them."

I smiled and led her out to the truck. As I started the engine, I was feeling pretty good about the surprise I had planned for Ellie, but just to be safe, I took my time driving back to the house. When we finally pulled up in the driveway, I was relieved to see that the guys were already gone. As we started inside, Ellie turned to me and asked, "Is something going on?"

"Why do you ask?"

"I don't know. It seems like something's been on your mind all day. I was just wondering if everything was okay."

"Everything's fine." After I opened the front door, I said, "I *do* have something to show you though."

"Is it something bad? Because if it's something bad, then I really don't want to see it right now." She barely had a chance to catch her breath before she continued, "It's just that today was such a good day, and I don't want to ruin it. I want us to just be able to—"

"Ellie."

"Is it bad?"

"No. It's not bad." I took her hand and led her over to the row of windows that faced the ocean, and just as I'd hoped, there was now a roomy porch with wrap-around seating along the wooden rails. There was also a large fire pit in the center to keep us warm on those cold winter nights. "Well? What do you think?"

"Diesel! It's unbelievable. How did you do all this?"

"Guardrail and the guys did it today while we were gone."

"When did you have time to ..." Her voice trailed off while the wheels started turning in that head of hers.

"Do you remember that first night I brought you here? We were looking out at the ocean, and you said if I built a porch out here that—"

She stopped me mid-sentence. "I would never leave."

"Exactly. That's why I left that night to go to the club-house. I went to work the details out with Cotton." I pulled her towards me and continued, "Did you mean what you said?"

"About never leaving?"

"Yes."

"You didn't have to build that porch to get me to stay, Diesel. I love you, and you alone are enough of a reason for me to stay."

"I'm glad to hear that, because I love you, too, angel. And I want you here with me. I want to make you happy."

"You already do. Just by being *you*."

ELLIE

Two months later

I'VE NEVER BEEN one to put a lot of stock in counseling, dredging up and then talking about all the bad things that have happened in one's life, but I was wrong. After just a few sessions with my therapist, Dr. Annette Jelks, I was already feeling better about myself and coming to terms with the nightmare that was my past.

Dr. Jelks was older, in her mid-sixties or so, and she dressed a little bit like a hippie with her long, flowy dresses and gaudy jewelry. I liked her smile and the purple tint in her gray hair. Yes, she was a bit eccentric, but I felt at ease from the first moment I met her, even though it took some time for me to truly open up. Other than Diesel, and until recently, my parents, I hadn't spoken to anyone about my past, but with each session, it became easier. She listened to me without judgment, even when it was deserved, and didn't provoke any conversations that I wasn't ready to talk about. When I felt that the time was right, I disclosed some of the awful things that Brady had done to me; she let me take things at my own pace, never interrupting me or leading me in another direction. She encouraged me to get out everything I needed to say, and once I was done, she would always ask the same question —just like she'd done during my latest session.

I had just finished telling her about the night I'd gone to the bar with Kelley, a friend of mine from the coffee shop for simply one quick, little drink. I came home a few minutes late, but Brady was furious when I walked in the door. He never liked me talking to anyone, much less making an *actual friend*, and to punish me for going against him, he beat me and then shoved me in a closet. Brady left me there for over twenty-four hours, and when he finally released me, he beat me again for making a mess in the closet.

As soon as I finished describing what had happened to me, Dr. Jelks picked up her pen and asked, "How did that make you feel?"

I thought it was an absurd question, but as always, I still answered, "I felt humiliated and angry. I hated him for doing that to me."

"I assume that you weren't able to discuss those feelings with him."

"I tried at first, but he never really listened; after a while, he'd become so angry if I tried to bring it up that we'd start fighting all over again," I scoffed. "I just learned to keep my mouth shut and avoid him as much as possible."

"That must've been very hard on you."

I knew what she was doing, but I took the bait. "Yes, it was, but he would be better for a while ... even nice. But it never lasted. It was a vicious cycle."

"Most cases of domestic violence are just like what you've described. After an attack, the aggressor feels guilty, and that remorse hangs around for a while. But inevitably, something always triggers the anger."

"I tried not to provoke him. I tried to do everything the way he would want it, but I couldn't seem to do anything right."

"I learned something a long time ago, Ellie, and it was a hard lesson to learn. You can't change other people. You can only change yourself. There was nothing you could do or say that would stop Brady from behaving the way he did. It only stopped when you decided to stand up to him. You gathered your courage, you faced your fear, and in the end, you got away from him. You changed the direction of your life because *you* were brave enough to make the change in yourself."

"So, it wasn't just me? You really don't think Brady could've ever changed?"

She studied me for a moment before she continued, "There are therapists out there who would disagree with me, but I truly think that there are some people who just can't be helped. I believe Brady is one of those people, but you, on the other hand, you have already made insurmountable changes. And I think those changes have been for the better, don't you?"

"I think so. I'm happier than I've ever been. I have my family back. I even talked to my brother the other day."

"I'm pleased to hear that you were finally able to reach him. How did that conversation go?"

"Really well, actually. As you can imagine, we had a lot of catching up to do."

"That's good to hear." With a hopeful tone in her voice, she asked, "And your folks? How are things going with them?"

"It's taking some time to get used to having them back in my life. For so long I was on my own, not having anyone who really cared about me, and now it seems like I have two families. But I love it. I wouldn't trade it for anything."

"And Scotty?" When I smiled, she raised your eyebrow and said, "I take it things are going well with him."

"Yes. Very much so. He makes me happier than I ever thought possible."

"Have you two talked about the possibility of having a family down the road?"

"He wants children, but I'm not sure. I don't think I could go through it again. If I lost another child, especially his, I think it would destroy me," I confessed.

"You're stronger than you think, Ellie. Don't ever let fear stop you from your dreams. A child can be a wonderful blessing. I'm sure you remember the feeling of being pregnant, having a little part of yourself growing inside of you and the love you felt for that child. I know it was difficult for you to lose her, but don't let that stop you from trying again. If the time comes when you are ready for a child, then you'll know it."

Like always, she's helped me see things from a different perspective. "Okay. Thank you."

"That just about does it for our session today. Same time next week?" she asked as she stood up.

As I followed her to the door, I said, "Yes. That will be great. Thank you so much."

When I got downstairs, Diesel was waiting for me. The weather had finally warmed up, so I wasn't surprised to see that he took the bike. He loved riding that crazy thing. I loved riding it, too, mainly because it gave me an excuse to be close to him. When he saw me walking in his direction, he grabbed my helmet and offered it to me. "How'd it go?"

"Good." I climbed on and sat down behind him and asked, "Where are we going?"

"I thought we'd shoot over to the hospital to see Liv and the baby, if that's okay with you."

"I thought they would be home by now."

He gave me a slight shrug. "I don't know about all that. I just know they're still at the hospital, and since we're right here, I thought we'd visit them. But we can go some other time—"

"Now is great. I would love to meet little Casey."

As soon as I put my helmet on, Diesel pulled out onto the road and started driving towards the hospital. I hadn't held a baby since that night, and I was feeling a little anxious. I didn't want to have a breakdown in front of Liv or his brothers, but I knew it was important to Diesel that we go. It was important to me as well. Over the past few months, Diesel's brothers and their wives have become my family, and I loved each and every one of them. I wanted to be there to congratulate Liv and Clutch, so I swallowed my anxiety and followed Diesel to their hospital room. When we walked in, Clutch was holding Casey in his arms while Liv slept soundly. He was so proud that it looked like he might burst right there on the spot.

His voice just above a whisper, Clutch said, "Hey, brother. Get your ass over here and see my beautiful daughter."

Diesel eased over to him, trying his best not to wake up Liv, and as soon as he got a look at Casey, a huge smile crept over his face. "She's just beautiful. Thank God, she looks like her mother."

"You wanna hold her?"

"Well, yeah. Why do you think we came over here?" Clutch gently lowered his daughter into Diesel's arms. "She's so tiny."

"She weighed in at seven pounds two ounces, and she's twenty-one inches long," Clutch boasted.

I looked at Diesel with that baby in his arms, and when I saw the tender look in his eyes, my heart melted. He lowered his lips to her head and kissed her lightly as he whispered, "Hey there, pretty girl. I'm your Uncle Diesel."

"Can you believe it, man? I'm a father."

"I know. It's freaking me out just a little." Diesel teased. "And to think that Smokey's next. Damn."

"He's not gonna know what to do with himself," Clutch told him. "There's no other feeling like this. It's gonna blow his mind."

"She really is a doll, brother. You did good."

"Thanks. I think so."

Diesel looked over to me and asked softly, "You wanna hold her?"

I'd been keeping it together pretty well, and I didn't want to take the chance on losing it, so I told him, "No, that's okay."

"You sure?" He walked over to me. "She's a real beauty."

As soon as I saw her up close, I knew there was no way I could turn him down again. "Okay."

Diesel carefully placed her in my arms and smiled. "Yeah, we're definitely gonna have to have a house full of these."

I looked down at her precious, little fingers and her tiny button nose, and I was overcome with an emotion I hadn't expected. Her smell. Her innocence. The way she felt in my arms. Holding her didn't give me a feeling of sadness or regret. Instead, I felt joy—pure and absolute—*joy*. While holding Casey didn't make me want to have a child *right now*, it did make me realize that the possibility was there. I looked over to Clutch and said, "She's perfect. Positively perfect."

"Thanks, doll." He smiled warmly. "How are things with you? Anything new going on?"

"Everything's great. I've been going to counseling every week, and I really like Dr. Jelks, my therapist. It turns out that seeing her was the best thing that could've happened to me. She's helped me a lot."

"That's really good to hear."

"I've also signed up for some summer classes, so I'll be going to school part-time and working at the coffee shop. I'm really excited about it."

"That sounds pretty awesome, Ellie. Glad everything's heading in the right direction for ya."

"I couldn't have done it without all of you, especially Diesel." I looked over to him and smiled. "He's been really wonderful."

"You got yourself a good one with him."

"Yes, I did."

I looked back down at the baby one last time before I walked her back over to her father. As I lowered her down into his arms, I said, "You better get yourself prepared. She's going to be a real heartbreaker."

"Oh, man. I don't even wanna think about it." Clutch shook his head. "We're gonna have to get busy. She's gonna need a little brother who can look out for her."

"Don't even think about it," Liv mumbled with her eyes still closed. "I'm gonna need some time to rebound before we start trying for another one."

A smirk crossed Clutch's face as he whispered, "We'll give it a couple of weeks or so."

"Clutch!" Liv warned.

"I'm just kiddin', babe. *Well, kind of.*"

Diesel chuckled as he said, "The club's gonna be overrun by babies before it's all said and done."

"Yeah, seems that way." Clutch agreed.

"I better get my girl home," Diesel announced. "Looks like we have some catching up to do."

I gave him a scornful look. "Umm … what?"

"Don't worry, angel. We'll just be practicing for now."

Ignoring him, I turned to Liv and Clutch and said, "If you guys need anything, just let us know. And congratulations. Casey is a beautiful little girl."

"Thanks, Ellie," Liv replied. As she pointed to Diesel, she said, "Keep that one in line."

"I'll do my best."

Just as we were walking out, Clutch called out to Diesel. "Hey. I forgot to tell ya. Cotton got the word from Gus. Everything with the route went as planned."

"I never had any doubt." Diesel smiled as he followed me out the door.

It was late by the time we got home, so after a quick dinner of sandwiches and chips, we showered and went straight to bed. It had been a long day, but unlike Diesel, I wasn't sleepy. I rolled over and stared at him, lying there looking so peaceful, and I just couldn't help myself. I inched closer to him and started trailing light kisses along the curve of his neck while my hand slowly roamed across his chest. When my fingers reached his lower abdomen, his eyes crept open. "Whatcha got on your mind, angel?"

"I was just thinking about what you said earlier."

"And what was that?"

I continued to nip and suck along his neck and shoulder as I mumbled, "I don't know ... Something about us practicing ..."

"Is that right?"

"Umm-hmm."

I lowered my mouth to Diesel's, and as soon as my lips touched his, his hands reached for the back of my neck. His fingers tangled tightly in my hair as he took control of the kiss. My hips automatically rocked against him, feeling him thicken beneath me while he devoured my mouth. The desire I felt for him was running rampant as he moved his hands to the hem of my t-shirt and pulled it over my head. He let out a deep breath as he took my bare breasts in his hands, holding them firmly while he lowered his mouth to my sensitive flesh. I loved the feel of his hands on my body—every touch, every flick of his tongue—sent me soaring to a new level of ecstasy. His erection throbbed against my thigh, and I was quickly becoming desperate to have him.

"We can practice any time you like, sweet angel. Any time you like."

"Please, Scotty," I pleaded.

A hiss escaped his lips as I reached down, slipping my hand into his boxers. Having my fingers wrapped around him, Diesel's breathing became short and strained; in a matter of seconds, I was flipped around and deposited flat on my back with the weight of his body pressed against mine. His mouth dropped to my ear, the warmth of his breath sent chills down my spine when he growled, "*Mine.*"

I loved the feeling of being claimed by him—I was his and he was mine. Suddenly, my panties were sliding along my skin as he eased them down my legs. A deep moan rumbled through his chest as he gazed down upon my naked body. My pulse quickened, and a devilish grin spread across his face. My entire body trembled with need as he settled his hips between my legs. Lowering his face to my neck, the bristles of his beard started tickling me as he licked and sucked along the contours of my body. Oh, how I loved this man. Heart and soul. I couldn't get enough of him. My hands dropped to his waist, pulling at his boxers, and seconds later they were on the floor next to his abandoned t-shirt. Even after months of being with him, I still marveled at just how handsome he really was. Every inch of him was like some kind of dream, and just like the first time, I wanted him more than I thought possible.

"I love you, Scotty."

"And I love you, too, angel."

I wound my hands around his neck, pulling him closer

and kissed him. It was gentle and slow, then I looked at him and whispered, "Mine."

"Fuck," he groaned when his hand slipped between us. Each movement was meticulous and slow, causing me to writhe beneath him while his thumb brushed back and forth. I was unable to control the sounds of my pleasure as he delved deeper inside me, not recognizing my own voice echoing through the room. I was completely lost in his touch, loving the feel of his calloused hands against my body. The bed creaked as I arched my back, feeling the muscles in my abdomen tighten with my impending release. My breath caught in my throat as waves of pleasure rushed through me, and just when I thought I couldn't take it a moment longer, he grazed his erection against my entrance. I gasped loudly as he thrust deep inside me, giving me all he had in one smooth stroke.

His hands reached up, fisting my hair as he drove into me again. Slow and demanding. His teeth raked over my nipples, and I cried out wanting more. I loved how he felt pressed against my bare skin, buried deep inside me. I never wanted to leave that spot. I couldn't get enough of him, and something told me that was how it would always be with him. I'd found him—the missing piece of my soul, and I would hold on to him, cherish him, and love him, until the day I took my last breath.

EPILOGUE

Diesel

Two Years Later

I WAS BARELY COMING TO, when I heard Ellie scrounging around in the kitchen. I rolled over to check the time and saw that it was too early for her to be up, much less making that kind of racket. I threw the covers back and pulled myself out of bed, heading into the kitchen to see what she was up to. When I walked in, she'd already started putting up the decorations, and the stove was covered with pots and pans. She was as busy as a fucking bee and had no clue I'd even walked into the room. "It's six thirty in the morning, Ellie. What in the hell are you doing up so early?"

Without turning to look at me, she answered, "Everyone will be here in a few hours."

"They won't be here until one."

"I know! That doesn't give me much time." She fussed about.

Today was not only our Clayton's first birthday, it would also be the first time that we were having everyone to the house. While my brothers have been over to hang out, and her parents, too, they'd never all been here at the same time, and she wanted everything to be perfect. Knowing that she was nervous, I walked over to her and pulled her into my arms. "Everything'll be great, angel."

"I know, but I can't help myself. I just want it all to be perfect."

"And it will be, but you don't have to do this all by yourself." I kissed her on the temple and said, "Let me take a quick shower, and I'll come help you get things ready."

"Okay." When I started towards the bedroom, she called, "Don't forget that you need to go get the cake."

"I know."

"And ice!"

"I know."

"And you might wanna grab some more cups and plates while you're out."

"Just make me a list. I'll get whatever we need."

"Thanks, babe."

"It's what I do, angel." I chuckled as I went to take my shower. By the time I was done, Clayton was awake, and Ellie had him sitting in his highchair eating Cheerios. As I walked over to them, it still amazed me how much our son looked like his mother. They shared the same dark hair and eyes, and when that boy smiled, he could light up an entire room. "Good morning, pot-squally. Your momma wake you up, too?"

He answered with a stream of incoherent babble, but I understood him perfectly, or at least, I pretended that I did. "I know, but keep in mind, she's doing all this for you."

He smiled, and Cheerio goo came oozing out of his mouth. I kissed him on the top of the head and grabbed my keys off the counter. "You got my list?"

As she handed me a slip of paper, she answered, "Yep. This should do it."

"I was only gone for twenty minutes, and my list has doubled."

"And?" She smirked.

I leaned towards her and kissed her. "It's a good thing I love you like I do."

"Ditto." She winked. "Thanks for helping me."

"Not a problem. You know that." As I headed for the door, I said, "I'll be back as soon as I can. Leave the balloons for me. I don't want you climbing up on that ladder."

"Okay."

I could tell from the sound of her voice that she wasn't listening, so I warned, "I mean it, Ellie."

"*Okay*. Fine. I'll wait."

I ran all the errands for Ellie, and when I finally made it back to the house, I walked in and found Two Bit standing on a ladder. He was hanging up the balloons while Zoe helped Ellie set the tables. Carrying the bags of ice over to the freezer, I said, "Hey, Two Bit. How's it going?"

"Better now." He got down off the ladder and handed me a handful of balloons. "Here ya go, buddy."

"*Seth*," Zoe complained.

"I didn't say I wasn't gonna help."

I looked over to Ellie and said, "I thought you were going to wait until I got back before we did the balloons."

"I said I wouldn't get on the ladder." She chuckled. "You didn't say anything about Two Bit."

Zoe walked over and gave me a wink. "She got you there, big brother."

"Don't encourage her, Zo."

"I can't help myself." She walked over to Clayton and carefully lifted him out of the highchair. "I can't believe my nephew is already one. How did that happen?"

"I can't believe it myself. This year has flown by." I walked over to them and as I looked down at my son, I asked, "So, when are you and Two Bit gonna get yourselves one of these?"

"It's not like we can run down to the supermarket and pick one up." She huffed.

"I know where they come from, Zo. Trust me." I chuckled.

"Well, if you must know…" She whispered and continued, "We've been trying for a while, and I think it finally paid off … *but you can't tell anyone, Scotty.*"

"Wait. Are you telling me you're pregnant?"

I was still trying to get over the shock of her news when I heard Two Bit fuss from across the room. "I thought we weren't gonna tell anyone yet."

"We're not. I'm just telling Scotty!" She argued … weakly.

"Tell him what?" Ellie asked.

"See what you just started," Two Bit grumbled. "It's on you when the whole club knows before sundown."

Shaking her head, Zoe turned to me and Ellie and said, "It's really early, and we don't want to jinx anything."

"We totally understand. Your secret is safe with us," Ellie assured her as she gave her a hug. "Congratulations though, that's great news! Promise you'll let me know if you need anything."

"Thanks, Ellie. Now, what else do you need me to do?"

Once we finished putting up the decorations, I took a step back to check it all out, and the house looked amazing. As soon as we tied the knot, Ellie had taken it upon herself to fix the place up. She even hung some of the paintings she'd done in her art class, and we'd bought a few new pieces of furniture. I was glad we finally had a chance to show it all off, and I knew she felt the same. Once my brothers and their families arrived, Ellie started to relax. The girls gathered around in the kitchen, making themselves busy as they gossiped about this or that, while the guys piled up in the living room with the kids. I smiled as I watched Cotton try to manage controlling the remote with his twin daughters in his lap. I had to give the man credit. He was determined as he flipped the channels to find the football game we were all dying to watch, and when he finally found it, the sounds of my heckling brothers filled the room.

When her folks finally arrived, Ellie left her spot in the kitchen and rushed over to them, giving them each a hug. "I'm so glad you both could come."

"We wouldn't miss it." As her father stepped out of the way, he revealed a man standing behind him. Even with the distraction of his fatigues, I could see the family resemblance and knew right away it was her brother. "We brought a little surprise for our grandson."

Ellie rushed through the door and wrapped her arms around him, screeching, "Joseph!"

"Hey, sis." He lifted her off the ground as he hugged her tightly. "Damn, it's good to see you."

"Why didn't you tell me you were coming?"

"We wanted it to be a surprise."

As he put her down, Ellie looked up at him and asked, "How long will you be home?"

"At least a few months. Maybe more. Just gotta wait and see how things play out," he explained. "Now, where's my nephew?"

"He's inside. Come on in and meet everyone."

After all the introductions were made, everyone started to settle in. As I'd hoped, Ellie's family fit right in, and with all the food everyone had brought, it didn't take long for the guys to start fixing their plates. While the kids ran amok, we stood around talking and eating and simply enjoying each other's company. It was a perfect day, and as I looked around the room at my brothers and their families, and Ellie with our son on her lap, I couldn't imagine a more beautiful sight. Family. That's what it'd always be about.

The End

More from the Satan's Fury Memphis Charter coming soon!

(Excerpt from Two Bit: Satan's Fury Book 7 after acknowledgments.)

ACKNOWLEDGMENTS

Natalie Weston – Thank you for all you do. I can't tell you how much your help means to me. I love you, chick. Even when I'm at my worst, you have a way of making me smile. And thank you for helping me sort through all the hot, sexy men to find the perfect cover. I know it must be so difficult. I can't wait for them to see what we have picked out for Fury's Memphis boys! Wowzer!

Ena and Amanda from Enticing Journey Book Promotions- Thank you for all you do. You guys rock!

Lisa Cullinan – As always, you are awesome. Even when you're super busy, and constantly editing a new book for me, you always find the time for me. Thank you so much for all you do. I owe you so much!

Tempting Illustrations – Thank you for your amazing teasers. I loved them all! If you're looking for some amazing teasers, be sure to check them out. http://www.temptingillustrations.com

Neringa Neringiukas –I can't thank you enough for sharing my book and teasers, and all of your kind words of support. Your friendship and kindness means so much to me. Thanks for being awesome.

Terra Oenning, Amy Jones, and Daverba Ortiz- Thank you for posting my books on teasers. It truly means so much to me that you take the time out of your busy day to sharing my work. You are all awesome.

Tanya Skaggs and Charolette Smith- Thank you for reading Diesel early and helping me make it even better. Your support means so very much to me.

Wilder's Women – I am always amazed at how much you do to help promote my books and show your support. Thank you for being a part of this journey with me. I read all of your reviews and see all of your posts, and they mean so much to me. Love you big!

A Special Thanks to Mom – I want to thank you for always being there and giving me your complete support. You are such an amazing person, and I am honored to call you my mom.

EXCERPT OF TWO BIT

Two Bit

TWO BIT-PROLOGUE

I grew up the youngest of four brothers. I was strong-willed with a mouth to match and wasn't afraid of anything. I owed my charming personality to my three wise-ass brothers. Being the smallest made me an easy target, so they took every opportunity to make my life a living hell. I had to get tough. They gave me no choice. I learned early on if I wanted something, especially where junk food was concerned, I had to be prepared to fight for it. Deep down I liked the way things were. Living with them made me stronger and more prepared to take on the world, but being the youngest wasn't my only obstacle. I was different from my brothers in every way. Unlike them, I wasn't very good at school, sports, or following rules. They were choir boys, doing what was expected and kissing ass, while I was busy looking for some kind of trouble to get into. I was always on the hunt, and when I found an old, beat-up Harley, I knew I'd found what I was looking for. Even though my family disapproved, I saved every penny I earned working part-time as a mechanic and bought it. Until then, I'd never felt passionate about anything. I spent an entire summer bringing her back to life, and I'd never felt prouder than the day I rode her for the first time.

My folks always hoped I'd follow in my brothers' footsteps, but none of the heartfelt lectures or parental threats ever stuck. I had no desire to sit in some office the rest of my life, so I set out for something different. My parents weren't happy that I wasn't heading off to college, especially my dad. He pulled out all the stops, thinking if he pushed hard enough that he could change my mind. He gave me one ultimatum after the next, but I didn't waiver. I knew then I wanted something more than a mundane life working nine-to-five in some office, then coming home to my two and a half kids. It was what was expected, but it just wasn't for me. I wanted something different.

Determined to find my way, I started working full-time at the shop and moved into one of the apartment upstairs. I worked my ass off, staying after hours and on weekends, until I saved enough money to buy myself a 2007 Harley Softail. With the few clothes I could stuff in my saddlebags, I hit the road. It was a decision that would alter my path in ways I couldn't begin to comprehend.

After a week of traveling from town-to-town, I'd found myself in a small bar on the outskirts of Clallam County. It was like any other run-of-the-mill bars I'd ridden by, but something about it caught my attention. Maybe it was the flashing cold beer sign or the various motorcycles parked out front, but something about it drew me in. Unaware of what I'd find inside, I walked through the front door and headed straight for the counter. Several bikers from the Satan's Fury MC were sitting there with their beers, talking. They were seemingly unfazed that I'd approached. I'd heard my fair share of stories about the notorious biker club, but seeing them firsthand made me curious to know more. I ordered myself a beer and couldn't help but eavesdrop as they conversed back and forth.

"The asshole pulled right out in front of me," a man with a dark beard growled. He was covered in tattoos and had a hard look about him—the kind that screamed "don't fuck with me". He took a slug off his beer before he continued. "Never even checked up until I pulled up to his window."

From the end of the counter, I heard one of them say, "Careless bullshit."

An older guy in his mid-forties to early fifties, leaned forward as he shook his head. "Common sense is all it takes, brother."

You know that thing that most people have that tells them to keep their mouth shut and mind their own damned business? Yeah, I didn't have it. My brain just didn't work that way. I said what was on my mind, whether it was a good idea or not. It's one of the reasons my dad always called me Two Bit; I was always throwing in my two cents whether it was warranted or not. Without giving it a second thought, I turned to them and said, "Problem is… most folks don't have common sense."

The men all turned and looked at me with their eyebrows furrowed. You'd think I would have turned away, tucked my tail between my legs, and shut the hell up, but I didn't. Hell no. I just kept running my mouth.

"They have their heads crammed too far up their own asses to even notice anything else."

"No doubt about that." The older guy gave me a questioning look. "You got a name, kid?"

"Seth Lanheart... but most folks just call me Two Bit."

"You ride, Two Bit?"

I nodded. "Since I was just a kid." I could've just stopped there, but I didn't. "There's nothing better. Just follow the basic rules, and life is good."

He paused as he studied me for a moment. "Care to share these rules of yours?"

"Pretty simple. Take care of your bike, use your head for more than holding up your fucking helmet, and respect the road because it can hit back harder than you ever could."

"Pretty good rules you got there, kid." He turned up his beer and finished it off before he stood up. The others followed suit and started for the door. Before they left, the older man turned to me. "You should come by the clubhouse sometime. If you're up for it, we might be able to put you and your rules to use."

Even though I had no idea where their clubhouse was, I replied, "Maybe I'll do that.."

"When you get to the gate, tell him Cotton sent ya."

TWO BIT

"*You* ready to roll out?" Clutch asked, sounding impatient. I could tell by the look in his eyes that he was set to go and ready to get our run over and done. While he'd never complain, I knew he was like many of the other brothers. He had his woman waiting for him at home and didn't like the thought of leaving, even if it was just for one night. It was one of the sacrifices that had to be made to keep the club running.

"I'm always ready, brother. Just say the word."

"Have you seen Stitch or Q'?"

"They're waiting out back. Let me grab my shit, and I'll meet you there."

He nodded and started for the back door while I headed down the hall to my room. As I grabbed my duffel bag, I felt a sense of accomplishment. Over the past year, everything in my life had come full circle. After I got my in with the club, I spent the next year and a half prospecting, getting to know the ins and outs of the brotherhood, and ensuring my place in the club. It wasn't always easy. I worked my ass off, did whatever I was told, and learned when and when not to open my fucking mouth—which ended up being one of the hardest lessons I had to learn. It took a lot of blood, sweat, and tears, but I eventually proved my value and got my vote. It'd all been worth it. Getting my patch was one of the best days of my life. I'd found my place, worked for it, and earned it. It was an honor to stand beside my brothers and call them family.

When I walked out the back door, Stitch was already on his bike while Clutch and Q' were waiting in the SUV. As the club enforcer, Stitch had always been quick on the draw, prepared to handle anyone or anything that crossed his path, but patience wasn't exactly one of his strong suits. Knowing he wasn't a man who liked to be kept waiting, I hurried to my bike and followed them out the gate. The sun had already set and darkness had fallen as we headed towards the interstate, making it easier for us to travel undetected. These runs were nothing new. The club had been running guns for years, long before I started prospecting. Over the past year, we'd converged with several of Satan's Fury charters, creating a larger pipeline. This enabled us to move a larger shipments down south and get a bigger payouts. While at times it could be dangerous, gun trafficking had turned out to be a very profitable trade for the club, and our next shipment would be the biggest one to date. We were staying the night in Seattle so we could meet up with our distributor first thing in the morning. Once we got the load, we'd meet up with the Seattle charter, and they'd make sure the goods made its way to Memphis.

When we got to town, Clutch led us to a small diner

so we could grab a bite to eat. As soon as we parked, we headed inside and found us a table in the back. It was your typical diner with red checkered tablecloths and the smell of hamburgers drifting through the air. Many locals were sitting around talking as they enjoyed their food. We each glanced over our menus, and when the waitress came over to our table, Q' was the first to place his order. "I'll have two burgers with everything, an order of loaded fries with extra cheese, a beer and... a piece of pecan pie."

Q' was tall and thin, which was surprising considering how much the guy ate. I'm six-foot-five and two seventy on the hoof, and that scrawny motherfucker could eat me under the table any day of the week. "Damn, brother. Where do you put it all?"

"What? I'm a growing boy," he scoffed trying to look offended.

"Sure, you are." I laughed as I turned to the waitress.

We each placed our orders. Once she had gone back to the kitchen, Clutch looked down at his watch and yawned. "I can't believe it's only ten. Damn. I'm wiped."

I smirked as I taunted him. "All those late nights are catching up with you."

He sighed. "Seems like there is always something going on. Charlie and his baseball and football... and Hadley with all her school projects. It's never ending."

"I hear ya, brother. I can't remember the last time I got a good night's sleep. Mia just started teething and wants us all to know she isn't happy about it," Stitch complained, but it was clear by the look on his face how much he loved his daughter. She was just a few months old, but she'd already wrapped her father around her little finger. He looked over at Q' and growled, "You better not snore tonight, numb-nut, or there will be hell to pay."

Laughing, he replied, "I'll do my best, brother."

We all grew quiet when the waitress came over to us with our food. Q' wasted no time digging in, and the rest of us followed suit. A half an hour later, we were done and headed back out to our bikes. As soon as we got to the motel, Clutch went inside to get our rooms sorted. After several minutes, he came back out and handed us each a key. "Q', you'll be with Stitch."

Stitch tossed his cigarette to the ground as he grumbled, "Like I said... no fucking snoring."

Shaking his head, Q' took his key. "I don't know what you're talking about, Stitch. I'm not the one who snores."

"Ah, yeah... you *do*."

"I haven't had any complaints."

With a cocked eyebrow, Stitch retorted, "You got yourself a woman?"

A shit-eating grin spread across his face. "Not a regular, but I have my fair share of the ladies."

"You want one to stick around, you best quit that fucking snoring." With that, Stitch headed towards their room. I grabbed a change of clothes out of my saddlebag and followed Clutch up the stairs. As soon as we stepped inside the room, Clutch dropped to the bed and threw his arm over his eyes. "Set the alarm for five."

"You calling it a night?"

"Hell, yeah," he grumbled. "Tonight will be the first night in weeks I'll be able to sleep without any interruptions."

After I set the alarm, I headed to the bathroom for a hot shower. Unlike the others, I wasn't tired; I needed help winding down. By the time I was done, Clutch was sound asleep. Trying my best not to disturb him, I lay down on my bed and started flipping through the messages on my phone. It didn't take long. I only had one. Like clockwork, my mother touched base every week to make sure I was still breathing. Once I'd let her know I was alive and well, I tossed my phone on the table beside the bed and stared into the darkness. I rolled to my side, trying to get comfortable, but I was too keyed up to sleep. Knowing I was just wasting my time, I got up and put on my jeans and t-shirt. After I pulled on my boots, I grabbed my wallet and stepped outside to smoke a cigarette. I'd just taken my first drag when I noticed a flashing neon sign across the street. Thinking a beer might help take off the edge, I headed down the stairs and across the street.

As my feet hit the gravel of the parking lot, I could hear the loud music blaring from inside. There were bikes and a few beat-up old trucks parked at the sides of the entrance. The front of the place was pretty well lit up, but it was pitch black all around the rest of the building. An uneasy feeling hit me as I walked through the door, but per my usual self, I ignored my better instincts. Seconds later, I found myself seated at the Nudie Booty Strip Club bar. I reached for my phone to leave Clutch a message, letting him know where I was, but realized I'd left it in the room.

A young waitress with short, curly blonde hair and way too much makeup came up to me with a seductive smile. She batted her bright blue eyes as she leaned over the counter, exposing more than a hint of cleavage. "What can I get for you, handsome?"

"A beer would be great."

"Draft or bottle, darlin'?" she purred.

"Whatever you have on tap will be fine."

"You got it." She sauntered over to the keg, filled my glass, then brought it back over to me. "Can I get you anything else?"

"This'll do it, thanks."

Her eyebrows furrowed as she studied me for a moment. "You're not from around here, are you? I'd remember a guy like you. You're not the kind of guy a girl would forget."

"Nope. Just passing through."

"You should stick around a little while. I get off at twelve."

"Sorry, doll. I'll be long gone before then."

"That's a shame." She ran the tips of her fingers across my arm. "I think the two of us could have a real good time."

"As much as I'd like to find out, it ain't gonna happen tonight."

"Well, maybe next time." She started to walk away, but stopped long enough to say, "Let me know if you need another."

"Will do."

While she was busy tending to a brute at the end of the bar, I took the opportunity to look around the room. While at first glance it seemed like your ordinary strip club with its scantily dressed waitresses and the strippers with large, fake breasts dancing on the stage, it was far from typical. Nudie's was run by the Chosen Knights. I hadn't realized it until I saw their motto: "Chosen by Fate. Bound by Honor".

Just reading it made my stomach turn. There was

nothing honorable about their Brotherhood. There was a time when they were a decent group of guys. They lived by the code—for family and what was right—but things changed when their long-time president died. Now, they were all about quick profit and didn't give a fuck who they crossed in the process. That was evident by the way they ran the strip club. The place looked like a dump with no real bouncers, and the girls looked high as kites as they paraded themselves on stage.

I should've used my head. I should've gotten up and left the minute I spotted their colors, but I figured it was just one beer—just a five-minute reprieve from the silence of that hotel room. I didn't see the harm. I didn't realize that the decision to come in to *this* strip club on *this* night would alter the course of my destiny yet again.

I'd gotten midway through my beer when I overheard one of the bikers behind me boast, "It'll be one hell of a score."

Another one replied, "Don't you know it. They'll never see us coming."

"Serves those motherfuckers right for doing business in our territory."

Trying to remain unnoticed, I took a slug of my beer and listened as one of them said, "It's been a long time coming."

"They know it's our fucking territory. Fuck. Everybody knows it, but they think they can just come in here and do whatever the hell they want without going through us first. Fuck that."

"I still say we end those motherfuckers," one of them grumbled. "I don't give a fuck who they are."

There was no way to be sure, but something in my gut

made me think they were referring to us. Just hearing them talk made my heart start beating out of control. I was torn between getting back to the hotel to warn the others and stick around to hear what else they were going to say.

"Fuck no. We gotta get in and get out."

"He's right. Killing them isn't an option. We just want to rattle them… teach them a fucking lesson and make them think twice before coming around here again—not bring on a full-blown war. At least for now."

"What makes you think stealing their shit from them won't bring on a war?"

"Oh, they'll want a war, there's no doubt about that. But they'll never know it was us. We'll make sure of that. Like Prez said: we go in with no bikes and no colors. Keep our mouths shut, and they'll never even know it was us."

Deciding it was time for me to get the hell out of there, I tossed a ten on the counter and started towards the door. I was just about to step outside when I heard a woman's voice say, "Back off, Slider."

My focus was immediately pulled to the side hallway where one of the bigger bikers, tall and muscled up like a linebacker, had a woman pinned to the wall. His hair was pulled back in a braid, and his thick beard was just a few inches from her face. The girl, a cute blonde with long, wavy hair and a killer body, was glaring at him like she was about to cut his throat. "You've got two seconds to get your hands off of me."

"Don't be like that, baby."

"Get this through your thick head! I'm not your baby. I'm not your anything. Now, get off of me, asshole." She gave him a hard shove, but he didn't budge.

I watched his hand drop to the curve of her full breast as he gripped her tightly. "This shit is getting old. I'm tired of playing games with you, bitch."

I cleared my throat, drawing both of their attentions in my direction. Her hazel eyes glistened as I took a step closer. "You okay?"

"I'm fine," she answered with a high-pitched voice. Her eyes were wide and filled with panic, making it clear that she wasn't. Strangely enough, she seemed more afraid of me than the guy pawing at her. "*Really*. I'm okay."

"You sure about that?"

"You heard her, asshole. Now, get the hell out of here before you and me have a problem," he growled as he looked daggers at me.

"See that's where you're wrong. We already have a problem." It probably wasn't the best idea to start something up with this guy, especially with his brothers sitting just a few feet away, but there was something about the girl—maybe it was the way she looked at me or the fiery sound of her voice. Whatever it was, there was no way in hell I was leaving her there with him—even if that meant taking a fall.

ZOE

It's not exactly every girl's dream to work at a strip club, especially one run by the Chosen. Actually, it's a nightmare—a nightmare I can't seem to escape. I had big plans for myself. I was going to go to college to be an accountant. I wanted a career and a family. I couldn't imagine anything better than coming home after work to find my kids waiting for me. I had it all planned out, but my father dying put an end to those pipe dreams. When I was just a toddler, right after my mother died, my father got a wild hair and decided to form a motorcycle club with a couple of his friends. I think when it came down to it, he was lonely and needed something to occupy his time. The guys named themselves the Chosen Knights, and my father, Lucky, was the obvious choice for president. What started as a small group of friends riding and enjoying the camaraderie of brotherhood quickly turned into something more. It didn't take long for others to become interested in joining their small group, and in a matter of a few years, they'd managed to acquire a clubhouse and a real name for themselves. Most of them worked blue collar jobs like mechanics, welders, and line workers. Eventually, they decided to pool their resources and open up a shop of their own. They were a family who worked hard and played even harder.

Made in the USA
Middletown, DE
10 January 2019